A Few Small Moments

This book is a work of fiction.
Any resemblance to any person, living or dead;
or to any place or situation, is purely coincidental.

Cover Art by Susan McClellen, Creative Media, University of Iowa

ISBN: 0615454127
EAN-13: 9780615454122

A Few Small Moments

SHORT STORIES

by

Carol Scott-Conner

Rachel Lord Press

For Harry, with love and gratitude

ACKNOWLEDGEMENTS

I want to thank the literary journals in which these stories were initially published. I appreciate the hard work of their editors and their editorial staffs. And I am deeply grateful for their confidence in my work.

"Masks" was first published in *The North Dakota Quarterly*.

"The Notebook" was first published in *From the Clinic (Blue Cubicle Press)*.

"Trauma Service" was first published in *Wisconsin Review*.

"Predators" was first published in *Buffalo Carp*.

"Clinic Day" was first published in *Amoskeag*.

"Who Will Catch Me When I Fall?" was first published as "Trauma Patient #35" in *The Griffin*.

"A Teaching Hospital" was first published in *The Listening Eye.*

"Trauma Patient #25" was first published in *The Coe Review.*

"The Ninth Life" was first published in a different form in *Willow Review.* It was included in the Iowa Summer Writing Festival 2010 Anthology.

"By the Book" was first published in *The Healing Muse.*

"Evening Rounds" was first published in *Taproot Literary Review.* It was included in the Iowa Summer Writing Festival 2009 Anthology.

"From the Heart" was first published in *The Healing Muse.*

CONTENTS

PREFACE

My life as a woman in surgery has been a tapestry of many small moments. Each moment, sad or happy, has been fraught with significance. These short stories derive from those small moments.

These stories are fiction. Nothing happened as depicted herein, but everything is true to the academic surgical life.

In 1981 I finished my general surgery residency at New York University College of Medicine and started my career as an academic surgeon. At that time, female surgeons were a distinct minority. It has been a pleasure to see their ranks expand over the decades that followed.

These stories were developed and refined during the Iowa Summer Writing Festival. To Amy Margolis and her staff, as well as to Wayne Johnson, Rick Hillis, Gordon Mennenga, Karen Subach, and innumerable other gifted writers, I owe all that is good in these tales. The flaws are purely my own. My thanks also to Bruce Brown MD, Terry Wahls MD, Kimberly Ephgrave MD, Bill Radl, and other members of the writing group at the

University of Iowa Carver College of Medicine for their support and guidance.

None of this would have been possible without the constant support of Harry Faulkner Conner MD MPH, my husband of almost 37 years, my best friend, my advisor and confidante. Legions of students, residents, patients, and colleagues all contributed in some measure to these tales.

Do not look for yourself as an individual in these pages, you are not there; yet each of you is everywhere, in everything that I do. You have all contributed to these "few small moments."

Carol Scott-Conner

Part I. From the Ivory Tower

MASKS

Clinical faculty had no tenure. Alix had known that when she took the job as Clinical Assistant Professor of Surgery. So now she'd have to find another job, and they would load up the U-Haul and move on. She had promised Mark that she would make it work this time. And she indeed had, until today in the OR. The last case of a long day. First the intern, then the scrub nurse.

The operation should have been routine. A diverting colostomy on an elderly farmer with an obstructing colon cancer. But she was edgy, because the family had been so worried. And the day had begun so strangely, with that encounter with the raccoon outside the parking lot. So nothing the intern did was good enough for her, and she kept correcting him, each small correction corroding his fragile self-confidence rather than building it.

"You're holding the scalpel wrong. Hold it like this," she had said, taking the blade away from him and demonstrating so fast that he hardly had time to react. "No, not there. Here." She shook her head.

His hands were trembling. He hunched low over the small incision.

"Stand up straight," she said. "Your head's in the way. I can't see."

He stood up, but didn't look at her. His eyes glistened. She remembered how one of her own professors had ridden her through every case. She had developed a trick – wearing her surgical mask high, just under her eyes, behind her glasses but loose to the skin, with a gap so the tears could run unnoticed, invisible, she hoped, behind the mask down to her lips where she'd lick them away. She had eased up a bit on him, relaxed, and things had actually improved.

But then, just as they were moving along well, a small artery spurted fresh red blood from the edge of the colon, and as Alix tried to expose it, it tore, almost retracting beneath the edge of the small incision. Into the belly, where it would be impossible to find without opening the incision much wider.

Keeping her eye on the bleeder, Alix held out her right hand, palm open, toward the scrub nurse and asked for a Halsted clamp. The nurse promptly slapped the clamp into her hand, and she put her thumb through the thumb-ring and moved her hand into the field, still watching the bleeder.

But as she spread her fingers to open the jaws of the clamp she noticed, just in time, the sharp teeth of a Kocher clamp rather than the delicate jaws of the Halsted. Teeth that would have shredded the fragile vessel, shortening the stump by a fraction of an inch and making control all that more difficult. And she had snapped.

Damn her impatience, and damn her hot temper, and damn that scrub nurse. Damn the OR nursing supervisor who had assigned an inexperienced scrub nurse and damn the residency program director for giving her a raw intern for what should have been a routine operation on a fragile old man.

They got the bleeder and finished the case, and she didn't have to open the incision any wider. The patient had looked good in the Recovery Room. But she had exploded. And she had been warned several times. Now all that the Dean needed to do was write a letter giving her one year's notice.

Alone in her office, she stood at the window and leaned on the windowsill. Fair weather this morning had given way to signs of an early winter, and now rain mixed with sleet slanted down through the darkness. A car turned the corner in front of the old part of the hospital and spun out, tail fishtailing.

"Steer into the skid," she muttered urgently, "steer into the skid." But the car kept slipping and came to rest, finally, crossways, tail against the stop sign. She turned away.

She felt a bluesy sense of panic.

She turned back to her desk. Pulled her parka over her white coat, turned out the lights, and set out for home.

* * *

Two hours later, Alix sat facing her husband across their battered old kitchen table.

She suddenly looked up from her dinner and said, "I saw a raccoon this morning."

Mark noticed that the left corner of her mouth was twitching slightly, that tiny tic betraying a high level of inner tension. She was always so controlled – he was sure that her hands never trembled in the OR – this twitch was the only outward signal of perturbation. Until she exploded. The tic would normally be hidden behind her mask, and maybe that was why it had persisted.

"Yes..." he said, and waited. The analyst's yes. Clear and even-toned, like the high tone of Mandarin Chinese, betraying nothing, going neither up nor down, but absolutely flat and level. Go on, that tone implied. I will listen. I won't judge.

"The raccoon was slinking along the curb like a cat. I thought it was a cat. Then I got closer and I saw the mask. It was standing over the body of a second raccoon, dead in the gutter, next to a storm drain. When I came closer it looked up at me with this ferocious anger. It stood there – planted four square – a fighting stance – and stared me down. I thought maybe the dead one was its mate, or baby or something..." She fell silent.

Could have been murder, he thought, but all he did was nod. He said, "What did you do next?"

"I crossed the street to give it some space. In case it was rabid, you know. Then I looked back and that raccoon was sniffing at the carcass...I almost thought it was going to start eating the flesh. Do raccoons cannibalize? Are they scavengers? They always seem so clean – they fish, they wash their food – but people say that's a misperception, they don't really do that..." She fell silent again and turned her attention back to her pasta.

He waited. There would be more. He thought about the summer they had spent in the Adirondacks when he was a kid, how the raccoons would get into the garbage. The clash of metal trash cans, the sound of the lids weighted with bricks hitting the gravel. Sometimes the cans rolled and rattled and clanged down the hill, scattering garbage as they went. Raccoons ate anything, he thought.

"I kept seeing that image all day," she said. "That fierce little face. The raccoon's posture – a real fighting stance. It must mean something. A kind of omen. You never see raccoons hereabouts in daylight. And it was completely lucid, not rabid, I could see tell by the eyes. And to see that today, this morning..."

She was superstitious, an odd admixture of child-like magical thinking and the objectiveness of the surgeon, as if she was able to tap into a hidden river deep in her consciousness. A source that most people lost access to at puberty. Carl Jung would have loved analyzing her. He had once found this endearing, but now he just wished she would tell him what was really wrong.

Once, when they were residents together, he had run into her in a back staircase of the hospital around midnight. They were both on call. His night had been busy – he had readmitted one patient in full-blown manic phase and a decompensated schizophrenic. When he had asked her how her night was going, instead of the usual litany, the accepted formulaic one-upmanship with which one resident typically greeted another, she had replied that she was fighting the Angel of Death. That she could sense the dark angel hovering over the hospital. No one would die that night, she said. She had looked feral.

ACHILLES HEEL

Alix visualized Dr Beth Abernathy's face on the boards as she lined up for her wheel kick. She felt her right bare foot pass cleanly through both boards; and, immediately afterwards, a subtle pop as her left Achilles tendon tore. Still turning, she slumped to the ground. Her Tae Kwon Do classmates stood frozen around her. She got to her feet and immediately fell again. Sterns, the senior black belt, was next to her by then.

"My left foot. It won't hold," she said, wondering at the absence of pain, the limpness of her left foot, the foot on which she had planted, pivoted, and turned, thus anchoring herself to break the boards with the knife-edge of her callused right foot.

Sterns took her foot in his hardened hands, moving it gently one way and then another. When he tried to push her toes back toward her knee, she cried out.

"Achilles tendon," said Sterns. She knew it already. Knew exactly what had happened, and why. Sterns said it first, "I've seen it happen before. You didn't warm up, did you? Didn't stretch?

You're not going to tournament with us, and you're sure as heck not testing next month. Only place you're going is the ER." He turned the class over to Jenn, the next senior black belt.

Jacob and Tim, twin orange belt Eagle Scouts, were at her side, eager to put their first aid skills to work.

"We can do a chair carry," Jacob said.

"It's easy. We just get our arms under your legs," Tim added.

"And behind your back."

"Not on your life," Alix said.

They compromised by splinting her ankle with rolled up newspapers and walking her, one on each side, over to the curb. Sterns pulled his Jeep up, and they loaded her in.

In the ER, there was considerable hilarity.

"Hey, look who's here, Ms Doctor Jackie Chan. What happened, someone finally kicked your ass? Nice splint, by the way."

* * *

Dr Beth Abernathy sat at the control desk in the ER, keeping tabs as two teams completed their workups of a man and woman brought in from a motor vehicle collision. Neither seemed very badly hurt, but both would be admitted overnight for observation. The EMT's had shown Beth a photograph of the couple's subcompact, and it looked like the car had taken the worst of the collision with the SUV.

The control desk was elevated on a platform that raised it approximately two feet above the level of the rest of the ER. So Beth had an excellent vantage point from which to watch the slight young woman limp in, supported on both sides by young orange belts. Alix. Wouldn't you know it. Alix, head hanging as she watched where she put her feet (and, no doubt, hoping no one would recognize her), passed on into an exam room without looking up.

It had been barely two days since that incident in the OR. Alix was on Beth's schedule for a come-to-Jesus meeting, as the faculty called it, tomorrow. Only three years earlier, Beth had recruited Alix to help out on the General Surgery services and to fill a position in the Trauma team.

Alix had excelled in her trauma fellowship at one of the most rigorous programs in the country, and yet she was fresh enough from her residency to retain an excellent grasp of the fine points of other areas of General Surgery. Perfect match.

But socializing Alix to the Department, to the Midwest, had been difficult. There had been a long series of complaints from patients, from coworkers, from nurses. Alix always had an explanation. She lost her temper when anything went wrong. Who could argue with perfectionism in a surgeon? Wouldn't you want your surgeon to insist on the very best from the rest of the team? To react promptly and, if necessary, loudly, to substandard behavior?

The OR was indeed stressful for everyone, and most surgeons managed to keep their cool. There was a clear line that delineated the appropriate response to that stress. Alix crossed that line, time and again.

Beth didn't look up later when she heard cubicle curtains pulled aside and the thump, thump, of someone tentatively walking out in a heavy plastic surgical boot, with crutches. Tomorrow's meeting would be interesting.

* * *

Late the following afternoon, Alix backed clumsily into the Minor Surgery OR, her scrubbed hands held higher than her elbows and dripping onto the tile floor. Her ankle ached. She wasn't supposed to be off crutches, but.... One more case, and then a meeting with Beth. She wasn't looking forward to it. Beth, the super woman. The Ice Woman, who never lost her temper in the OR, the surgeon who had hired her and now, most likely, was about to fire her. But that would be later. She needed to focus on the woman on the OR table.

"And so I called my doctor and he got me a mamm-ee-ogram," the patient was saying to no one in particular. A green cloth drape obscured the woman's face. Evidently the intravenous sedation had produced a disinhibition response, and she was talking freely.

Alix recalled seeing her in clinic – she had breast cancer. Was one of the Ice Woman's patients, in fact. Her BMI put her solidly into the "obese" category. She needed a port placed into one of the big veins draining straight into the heart, so she could undergo chemotherapy. Alix was the only one in the department doing these procedures under ultrasound guidance, an innovation that made the whole thing safer – or so Alix thought. Evidently Dr Abernathy agreed.

Alix tuned out the woman's recitation of all the events that had occurred after the mammogram. She clomped heavily over the table against the far wall where a sterile towel, gown, and gloves were laid out. She carefully dried her hands, opened the gown without touching the sterile outside and slid her hands into the armholes, pushing each hand out toward the cuffed wrist opening. This gown appeared to be an extra large. She pushed and pushed, and couldn't bring her hands close to the cuffs. Somebody's idea of a joke? Or maybe just carelessness. Sometimes it was difficult to distinguish the two.

Mildred, the Minor Room nurse, came up behind her and gave the gown a tug from behind, and Alix's hands slipped down to the cuffs. Soft new age music, Mildred's favorite, filled the small room. Alix preferred acid rock, but with the patient awake under local anesthesia, it would probably be a bad choice.

The task of putting on her sterile gloves occupied her for a moment, and she used this time to center herself, slowing her breathing, feeling her heart rate slow. She moved over the operating table, joined the resident, picked up a sterile marking pen.

"You're going to feel me touching you. I'm just making a mark... now I'm injecting some local anesthetic. This may sting a bit."

She was careful to work from the numb areas toward the periphery, so that the actual placement of the anesthetic was relatively painless after the initial stick.

Alix and her resident were the only people scrubbed. The relatively informal atmosphere of the Minor Room allowed a great flexibility in scheduling, but the tradeoff was that you really had no help in the sterile field. For operations like this line placement, it was ideal.

After she numbed the area, the resident tested the skin with a forceps, picking up and pinching tissue along the line marked for the incision, in order to make sure it was truly numb before making the first cut. Then Alix picked up the long needle, loaded it onto the syringe of local anesthetic, and probed with tip of the needle, seeking the easy path in. She found the big vein with her sterile ultrasound probe, watching the images unfold on the screen, seeing the image of the advancing needle.

"Ouch!" the woman said. "That hurt! It never hurt me when Dr Abernathy did my surgery."

Because you were asleep, you big cow. "Sorry." Alix injected more local anesthetic. Without taking her eyes from the sterile field, she reached out with her right hand to put the syringe and needle aside on the Mayo stand, a small moveable table that stood between her and the resident. She relaxed her grip, to set the syringe down, and felt a prick on the top of her right foot. She looked down to see that the syringe, tipped by a one inch long hypodermic needle, had fallen straight as a dart to lodge on the top of her operating shoe.

Like many surgeons, she wore white running shoes in the OR. Comfortable, easy to wash, but no protection from falling sharps. Too late, she recalled one of her professors saying, "Never wear sandals in the OR. Too easy to get cut by a falling knife." And it was her good foot, the right one in its running shoe; not the left foot, protected by its surgical boot. Why not the damn boot? Heavy plastic, would have deflected the needle. But no, she had been stabbed squarely in the instep of her good foot. A good stab, if she could believe what she had just felt. Had it drawn blood? She didn't know. Should she break scrub and wash the area? She flicked her foot and the syringe and needle dislodged and fell to the floor.

"Syringe and needle on the floor," she said mechanically. Mildred came over and retrieved the items. Alix tried frantically to remember if this particular patient was hepatitis B, or even worse, hep C, positive. She just didn't know.

Her resident stood poised, knife in hand, waiting the go ahead.

"Here, just where I've outlined," she said softly, and then more loudly, to the patient, "you're going to feel us touching you; you may feel some pulling and tugging. Let me know if we hurt you. We have plenty of local anesthetic."

On cue, Mildred dropped a fresh, unused sterile syringe and needle on the field. They went on with the case.

Half an hour later, the resident was closing the incision and Alix went out to talk with the family. The patient's mother, a plump and placid white-haired woman wearing a sweatshirt embroidered with a pair of cats, said, "She's determined to go home. We have a heifer turned on its calf. I told her well, then, if that's how you want it, then you just lie there and take it."

"She did indeed. Just local, it went very well. She'll be coming out in a few minutes. Here's my card, with the after-hours phone number on the back. Call if you have any problems."

Alix called Employee Health. There was a strict needle-stick protocol. It meant a trip to the other end of the hospital for a blood draw and a prescription for anti-retrovirals. No choice, she would be late. Again.

So, she called the The Ice Woman's office, and tried to ignore the tone of disdain in the voice of Beth's assistant when she learned that Alix would be late. Again. For a meeting with the Chair of Surgery, the great Beth Abernathy. Screw you, she thought, as she hung up the phone and picked up her crutches to clomp over to Employee Health.

* * *

The nurse on duty in Employee Health used to work on the surgical floor. A few months earlier, encounters with young surgeons, including Alix, had driven her to calmer waters. Nobody got too excited in Employee Health. Nobody cursed, nobody threw things. She recognized Alix instantly, and her lips moved into a semblance of a smile when the young woman came in on crutches.

She listened to Alix's account of the needlestick with a faint smile still on her lips. Passed the papers slowly across the desk to Alix. Stuck Alix twice for the baseline blood sample, and took her time finding the antiviral meds. She went over the instructions in a leisurely and thorough fashion, noting with some satisfaction that Alix seemed to be in an awful hurry. As usual.

"You need to come back in for a second blood draw. Here's the schedule. If you seroconvert, you'll be referred to Infectious Disease for treatment. In the meanwhile, here's a prescription for antiretrovirals, just in case," She looked the young surgeon straight in the eye.

Alix mumbled her thanks, nodded her head, and stood up with difficulty.

It was at least a city block back through the corridors of the hospital to Dr Abernathy's office and her hands and arms, un-used to supporting her weight on crutches, protested every step of the way.

* * *

It was after 5 pm when she knocked on Dr Abernathy's door. The old bat was sitting at her computer screen, typing away. She glanced up as Alix entered her office, then deliberately typed a few more words before turning her attention to the younger surgeon.

Beth motioned for Alix to sit in the chair facing the desk. A bad sign. The residents called it "the black chair" because it was lacquered black and bore the seal of the institution where Dr Abernathy had done her training. When Abernathy was in a good mood, and you were not on her wrong side, she had you sit over in one of a pair of wing chairs in the corner of the office. When she was pissed, you got the black chair.

"I was sorry to hear about your accident," Beth said.

Which one? Alix decided to play it neutral. "These things happen."

"More often to some than to others," said Beth. *What the hell did that mean?* Beth continued, "You know the old trauma saying – 'there are no accidents' – were you in a hurry?"

"Yes, I didn't want to be late."

"Rushing so much you forgot protocol, perhaps? Not watching where you put your used needle?"

That accident. "I always put my needles back on the corner of the Mayo stand, so no one gets stuck. This time, I misjudged the position of the stand, and..."

"Alix, it's late. Let me get right to the point. I have here three complaints – three incident reports – filed against you in the past two weeks. One for calling the head nurse on 2-south a 'slow fat ugly cow'..."

"She _is_ slow. My patient had to wait 30 minutes for morphine."

"A second for telling one of the pharmacists to 'bugger off' when he asked for your signature on a narcotics scrip..."

"I was with a trauma patient! I told him I'd get there as soon as I could,"

"That's not exactly how it was relayed to me. And three – this really boggles the mind – you threw a bloody Yankauer suction catheter at a scrub tech!"

"We were just finishing the suture line, deep in a hole. I asked for suction and she handed me a Yankauer with the tip missing. The sharp edge cut the suture. We had to redo the whole suture line."

Beth's old eyes narrowed in what might have been a sympathetic wince, showing, just for an instant, deep crow's feet at the corners, but then she continued, "I've warned you before. I've tried to mentor you, to help you along. I've opened doors for you just by giving you this job." Beth put both hands flat on her desk and leaned forward so suddenly that Alix, who had promised herself she would not flinch, that _she_ would own the mat in this sparring contest, blinked and pulled back an inch.

"Alix, you step out of line one more time and I swear I'll pull your hospital privileges so fast it'll make your head swim. I'm assigning you to Wound Clinic for the next two weeks. Some time debriding pressure sores might mellow you a bit. The rest of the team will cover your clinic and OR's. It's all taken care of. And I've arranged for you to get anger management counseling. Ten hours of it."

Beth stood up, and reflexively Alix stood up too, almost falling in her attempt to get up swiftly. She managed to catch herself and pulled her crutches over and eased them under her armpits, hanging her body weight on them as she had been told not to do, trying to stand upright for just a few more minutes.

"Remember, Alix, you're on a very short leash now. Don't make me regret I hired you. And please close the door on your way out."

* * *

Alone again, Beth stared at the closed door, listening to the clomp, clomp, clomp of Alix's booted foot as the young surgeon headed down the hallway to her own office. Beth had once been a brash young surgeon herself, fresh out of a rough-and-tumble Bellevue surgery residency. An older surgeon had taken her under his wings. She could still hear his voice in her ear, "You can't talk to people like that. Honey, you can't talk to people like that." She had changed. No reason Alix couldn't change either. Adapt. Grow. Develop. Take the next step. But then, some can, and some can't. Which was Alix?

Beth fidgeted with a heavy silver letter opener. A gift from some colleagues, years ago. She'd had to move several times to make it up the academic ladder. So many things had happened, so many changed over the years. Her husband had stuck with her, bless him, since medical school. She had heard that Alix and *her* husband — he was a psychiatrist, wasn't he? — were now separated. Everything that happened in the department – every good thing, and, especially, every bad thing – came to Beth's ears sooner or later.

* * *

Beth was in Breast Clinic the following day. A full slate – 20 patients – and a very welcome break from administering the department. She was a problem-solver by nature, one who craved the satisfaction of making a diagnosis and then bringing the case to closure. Fixing the problem and moving on. There were four new patients scheduled to be seen in Breast Clinic that day. Four problems to solve.

The first chart was marked "Staff only," meaning that the students and residents were not to see the patient. Beth noted that the patient was a young Pharmacy graduate student. It was not uncommon for students to be skittish about getting breast exams from trainees, or to prefer a female surgeon. These patients were routed to Beth.

As a young surgeon, eager to tackle the most technically demanding cases, following the trail blazed so clearly by generations of male surgeons before her, she had tried to limit the number of women with breast problems she would see. At some point she had realized this was a field where she could make a unique contribution. Made a virtue of a necessity. Now she couldn't imagine any other practice pattern. Breast by day, trauma by night.

With the clinic nurse at her side, Beth went in to examine this young woman. Her first impression was one of blackness. From under the generic grey-taupe poncho, black slacks and delicate sheer black stocking-shod feet protruded. Black sandals were neatly aligned next to the black Tommy Hilfinger bag. The woman's fawn-colored head scarf confirmed the impression of modesty. Her name was Soria, and she came from Saudi Arabia.

"Did you find the lump yourself?" Beth asked, after the introductory remarks were over.

"I found it when I was in the shower," she replied. Her voice was musical, cultured, with only the hint of a British accent. A BBC-type British accent. One could imagine her studying at Oxford, and, in fact, she had spent several years there.

"Show me where it is."

Soria raised her left arm and reached over with her right hand, felt around, "Here."

She fell silent as Beth's fingers probed the inner aspect of her left breast. There. Indeed. A firm, smooth nodule the size and texture of an acorn, but gently rounded at both ends. Mobile – her fingers chased it around its immediate neighborhood. Fibroadenoma. Breast mouse, the Brits call it for its propensity to skitter away from the examining fingers. She exhaled, not realizing she'd been holding her breath. Benign. All that remained was to prove it, without putting a surgical scar on this young woman's breast.

"It feels completely benign, Soria. I think it's what we call a fibroadenoma. We need to do two tests to confirm it. First, I want you to have an ultrasound of the breast. That will give us a good picture of its actual size and confirm that it is solid. Second, we'll do a fine needle aspiration for cytology to make sure it is benign, and finally, I'll re-examine you in several months."

She went on to explain how the fine needle aspiration and ultrasound would be done, concluding, "we could simply remove the mass, but it's not absolutely necessary. Any surgery I would do will leave a scar. Some women aren't comfortable living with a lump in their breast, even if they know it's benign. I don't know you well enough to know how you feel about this."

Soria hesitated. "I want it out," she said finally. "My roommate from Oxford has breast cancer. She's just my age. She's dying from it."

"OK, we'll take it out."

She visualized the placement of the incision, the location of the lump. Planned the operation in a split second. I'll do it through a circumareolar incision, she thought. In time, the scar will disappear, the eye drawn to the rose-tan of the areola, away from the lighter skin of the breast, the fine line dividing these. She pulled a pad of pre-printed forms from the rack over the desk, and drew her chair over to the exam table, so that Soria could look over her shoulder. Showed Soria the breast diagram.

"Here's the lump. Approximately. We'll make the incision here, and tunnel under the skin to here, and remove the lump. The scar will fade in time, and be hidden in the color change."

After explaining the procedure, she left Roberta to work out the scheduling details. Outside the exam room, she pulled out her pocket notebook. Affixed a sticker from Soria's chart, giving her full name, address, chart number. Made a quick sketch – just a semicircle to outline the pendulous bottom edge of a breast, drawn higher on one side, the lateral aspect. A circle for the areola, a dot for the nipple, and an ovoid for the mass, labeled it "?FA" and flipped the notebook closed. Back into her pocket. On to the next.

* * *

The Wound Clinic was in the oldest part of the hospital. In the past, when the team got a consult from the Wound Clinic, Alix simply sent a resident. Now she had a full day of wounds to deal with personally. Her first patient was there for his monthly pressure ulcer debridement. He had been shot five years earlier in a drug deal gone bad. Instantly paralyzed from the waist down, he had gained over 100 pounds since his "accident". Every month the ulcer got larger.

Alix dutifully photographed the ulcer and began working on the edges. The patient kept up a running stream of profanity.

There was a particularly nasty spot at the left hand rim. Alix had put peppermint essence on the outside of her surgical mask, but, rather than covering the odor of rotting flesh the peppermint had combined with it. A stronger and more repugnant mix had emerged, reminiscent of the taste of sugar-free mint gum after you have chewed it too long.

The clinic nurse sat charting meds on a computer terminal at the far end of the room. Her back was turned to Alix, and she had a "Big Gulp" container full of some icy beverage at her side. Alix could hear the faint swish of the icy slush whenever the nurse took a drink.

Alix suppressed the urge to swipe her gowned forearm against her sweaty forehead. Red blood ran suddenly from the edge of the wound.

"I need the Bovie."

The nurse kept on charting. Took another swig.

"Dammit, I said, I need the Bovie."

The nurse turned around, smiled, and got up ever so slowly. Put a grounding pad on the patient, being careful to check if he had any metal implants anywhere.

"Fuck, no," said the patient.

The nurse opened the sterile pack so Alix could get the electrocautery wand, holding it just slightly out of Alix's reach, so as not to contaminate the sterile field. Alix winced, leaned over on her bad foot, and struggled to remove the sterile wand. The nurse watched Alix struggle to keep holding pressure on the bleeder and simultaneously unfold the cord of the wand, pass it off the sterile field (again, the waiting hand ever so slightly out of reach), plugged it into the unit with painstaking care, and set the dial at 20.

Alix cauterized the bleeder. It kept on bleeding. Tried again, and again.

"What's the Bovie set on?"

"20"

"Well, put it on 35."

"Yes, doctor." The nurse smiled slightly and went back to her Big Gulp.

Six more hours to go.

The next patient had a small deep pressure sore over his sacrum. He'd been paralyzed in a car accident. His wife had been the driver, and she now devoted herself to his care. The other driver had been at fault, but leafing through the chart, Alix saw multiple notations from Social Services, "Wife reluctant to leave him alone," "Wife asks about stem cell transplants," and "Wife blames self."

The wife hovered over the wound now, watching Alix photograph it, pointing out areas of concern.

"Is it getting infected? It looks so red there."

"No, it's perfectly clean. The red stuff is healthy tissue. It's trying to heal."

Is it ever going to fill in?"

"Unfortunately, these ulcers rarely do. But he might be a candidate for a flap closure. A plastic surgeon could take tissue from here," (indicating the patient's buttock) "and move it to here. He's young and healthy, and you've kept it extremely clean."

Alix had the nurse call for a plastic surgery consult. They wheeled the young man into a smaller exam room to wait, covering his wound with a clean towel.

On to the next.

Sixty minutes later, one of the interns stuck his head in the door.

"Somebody wanted Plastics?"

"Somebody wanted a real Plastic Surgeon, not an intern."

"I'm supposed to see the patient and then call Dr McIntosh."

"You pick up that phone right now and tell McIntosh to get his fat ass over here or I'll go grab him by the balls and pull him away from his Botox clinic myself."

"Yes ma'am."

The nurse smiled and took an extra large swallow from her Big Gulp.

* * *

The tiled surfaces of the minor room reverberated like a gothic cathedral with the lilting strains of the "Waltz of the Sugar Plum Fairies". Sound spilled out into the small antechamber with the scrub sinks, lifting Beth's spirits as she adjusted her surgical mask before entering the small OR.

As Beth entered, Soria turned toward the door, and smiled. Soria lay flat on the operating table, her head scarf meticulously adjusted, and her body covered with sheets. Her slight form barely tented up the covers.

"Let me take a quick feel, refresh my memory," Beth said, expertly lowering the sheets and lifting the surgical gown to uncover just a small amount of territory around the areola, while keeping everything else covered. Preserving the illusion of modesty. Beth felt the lump. There. It hadn't gone away. We'll make the incision right there, she thought, and nodded.

As she worked, Beth could hear Roberta's voice on the other side of the drapes, murmuring, engaging Soria in conversation. Just as Beth's task was to do a workmanlike job of removing the lump and closing the incision, Roberta's task was to look after Soria, to monitor her vital signs, her comfort level, and to keep her distracted.

"Many people wonder why I wear the hijab, the veil. I have been asked if I am a novitiate – a nun – or if my father or my husband made me do it," Soria was saying to Roberta. "No one makes me do anything. I have studied in Oxford, at Harvard. Now I have come here to work in the best lab in the world, with people doing ground-breaking work in gender-specificity in pharmacokinetics. The hijab is my choice. It is a symbol. It protects me – a barrier between me and the world of sin. It goes back to the time when the prophet Muhammad's wives began to cover themselves in public, in order to command respect…"

It occurred to Beth that she was almost as thoroughly covered up as Soria. The only part of Beth that was exposed was a narrow band above her mask – her eyes and eyebrows, and another narrow band at her neck above the gown. Abruptly, Beth recalled a few lines she had written as a medical student:

> *The case goes badly, and I,*
> *masked and veiled,*
> *covered from head to toe*
> *like a Berber tribeswoman,*
> *am sent out*
> *to beg blood.*

She wondered if she still had the notebook at home with that poem. Third year of residency, what year would that be? She looked down at her hands, fingers curled around the Lahey clamps she was using to retract the edges of the wound. Right hand for precision, left hand for strength. The small joints in the fingers of her left hand ached briefly when she relaxed her grip. The knuckles had begun to swell about a year ago. Too many years of pulling, tugging, putting more stress on those joints than they were engineered to handle. She needed to find a different way to retract the tissue – shift the stress to another part of her hand.

There. The lump was out. Beth looked at it, felt it. Fibroadenoma, she thought with satisfaction. Let's see if the lab agrees. Closed the small incision, taking her time, enjoying the delicate movements, the way the tissue came back together, the precision, the flow.

* * *

Two days later, Soria's pathology report popped up in Beth's electronic inbox. Adenocarcinoma. Must be some mistake – but the gross description, size, shape, matched exactly. Beth went down to the lab to view the slides herself.

The pathologist on duty flipped the microscope lens to low power and started lecturing, "There – you see that cluster of cells? Doesn't look like the rest of the tissue – here, see, this is normal breast tissue? But these cells here, nuclear pleomorphism, mitotic figures, size, color, you see – it's all wrong. High grade, I'd say it's a grade III. Invasive."

"Estrogen receptors?"

"Sorry. We can't do receptors. The specimen wasn't processed properly."

"*What?*"

"We can't do receptors. We're outside parameters. The lump sat over the weekend in Formalin. We can't run the assay."

"Son of a bitch. That's NOT acceptable. This is a person we're dealing with, not a piece of meat that's gone past expiration date. Run it anyway."

"Can't do it. Get me some more tissue and I'll be happy to comply."

"There *is* no more tissue, you asshole. This lump is all there was. I can't plan the rest of her treatment without the receptors."

"Well, too bad. Next time use the established protocol."

Beth stood up, slammed the stool against the table holding the microscope, and stormed out of the small side room off the pathology lab. He was right, damn it. She had been so sure the lump was benign that she had failed to specify special processing.

She strode up the ramp to the operating room. This part of the hospital was a patchwork of buildings, floors at different levels all connected by sloping ramps. She'd taken this back hallway dozens of times, but this time she forgot about the small difference in level at the top of the ramp. The toe of her left operating shoe caught on the low projection. She became airborne for a brief moment, then landed heavily on her forearms, head bouncing as her chin struck the floor.

A passing medical student stopped to help her up, but Beth scrambled to her feet. Some kind of instinct. Don't show weakness. Checked her arms and hands. Everything moved, nothing was broken. Touched her chin. Blood.

There was a restroom down the hall, and she pushed the door open with difficulty. She was surprised to find that she was trembling. She had a profound urge to call her husband, to ask him to pick her up so she wouldn't have to drive home.

Looked in the mirror and saw a nasty gash just under the tip of her chin. Jaw wasn't broken, teeth were okay. She splashed water on her face and held pressure on the gash. It wouldn't need stitches, not if she could help it. She'd hold pressure and put ice on it for the next two days if she had to. Damned stupid accident.

The next day, Beth put on a thick turtleneck sweater and unfurled it to cover the gash. If she held her chin down, it just might do. At least, until she got to the OR. Her mask would cover it nicely. Good thing she had four cases on the schedule today. The wound throbbed. She had gotten little sleep, between the pain of the wound and her restless thoughts.

Central to all of it was Soria, Soria in her Hijab, with her faith and her clarity of vision. Soria with breast cancer, needing further treatment, treatment that would normally be directed by the results of those special stains. Stains that couldn't be done. That *wouldn't* get done unless Beth found a way to get them done.

She sat in her office with an ice pack on her chin, looking at a pile of incomplete manuscripts, thinking. Ten minutes until her first OR case started. Too early to start making phone calls to pathologists. But she had a plan. After the first case, she'd call the Pathology department head, her counterpart. Lay out the entire case. Together they would find a way to get the stains done. Maybe in one of the research labs. Then she'd call Soria.

* * *

At the entrance to the OR suite, she saw Alix clomping along on her crutches. Her exile to the Wound Clinic was over, but she was still getting around with difficulty. Their paths intersected at the heavy swinging doors.

Alix shot Beth a sidewise glare and kept going. These doors hinged outward, and Beth was virtually certain Alix could not make it through unaided. There was, of course, a touch plate to trigger and automatic door opener, but everyone ignored it. Beth paused for a moment.

"Here, let me," Beth said, and she held the door open for the younger surgeon. As Alix turned to look at her in surprise, she added, "Let's get a cup of coffee after we're both done in the OR. Unbridled anger is the Achilles heel of surgeons like us. I have some suggestions for you."

THE NOTEBOOK

Futo/Dare no sei demo nai/Aranami
By accident/no one is to blame but myself/rough waves.

Beth and Jonathan Abernathy sat at a table on the dock of the Captain Kidd restaurant in Woods Hole, Massachusetts. The surface of Eel Pond was lightly cat's-pawed by the wind, and periwinkle blue starched tablecloths on empty tables around them flicked briskly.

Beth capped her fountain pen and looked over at Jonathan. "Would you still love me if I weren't Chair of Surgery?" she asked suddenly.

"Even more. You'd probably be a *lot* easier to live with."

"The thing is, I just don't care anymore. And that's really bad. I'm thinking about getting out of surgery altogether. I could write poetry, maybe even go back to school."

"Oh Bethie, Bethie, you're just tired."

"True enough. I am that." She turned back to her notebook and began to write down the names of small boats passing out of

Eel Pond. They returned every summer at about the same time of year to this small seaside village where they had honeymooned 35 years earlier. Just before starting medical school. In time, Jonathan had matured into a cardiovascular researcher. Beth had developed an unexpected passion for surgery during her second year med school rotation.

For the past decade or so, she had run a moderate-sized Department of Surgery at Buckthorne University College of Medicine. Buckthorne was not a particularly wealthy university. Money to pay faculty salaries had always been tight, but for the last several years she had been working in crisis mode.

The waiter arrived with their salads. Jonathan cut his salad carefully into bite-sized pieces and sprinkled it with raspberry vinaigrette dressing. Beth set her notebook aside. Her fountain pen had left a splotch of blue ink on her middle finger, and she wiped that finger on her LL Bean denim skirt now, in a vain attempt to erase the stain. She looked at Jonathan.

"I went into the OR last week, and I couldn't remember the face of the woman I was about to operate on. She wasn't even a person anymore...when did that happen? Somewhere in the midst of all the budget meetings. All the worry about money to pay salaries," she said, fiddling with the callus on her thumb. "It's time to move on, I think."

"You think most people love their jobs? Most people just work. Few even get to choose. They think they're doing good just to have a job. We were lucky."

"Maybe. Ever wonder what life would be like if you were born someone else? Somewhere else?"

He shook his head. "I wouldn't be me. It's a meaningless question."

"But don't you ever wonder?" She lifted her gaze from the surface of the water and looked directly at him. The setting sun caught the hairs of his beard and his face seemed to be edged in gold. He looked as he had the year they met. He smiled and reached over and gently took her hand. His arms were almost twice as thick as hers, tightly muscled, not an ounce of flab anywhere, lightly freckled and thickly covered with red-gold hairs. His plain gold wedding band matched hers. He turned his wrist to glance at his black runner's watch.

She shifted in her chair, pulling her hand gently free, and said, "What have you been reading? What's new in the greater world of science?"

"Well, for one thing, they just found out that entropy isn't universal," Jonathan remarked.

"Sure it is. The three laws of thermodynamics: you can't win, you can't break even, you can't even get out of the game. We learned that in college physics."

"It turns out there is some kind of force that actually increases order, at the atomic level." He went on to carefully explain the detailed sequence of observations that supported this theory. "But time can't run backwards. Well, of course, it can at the subatomic level, but it can't really run backwards, because of causality."

Causality, she thought. The chain of events. It only goes one way. You can't take a scrambled egg, break it down into parts, reassemble it, and expect it to hatch. Can't make the ureter whole again if you accidentally nick it during a bowel resection. Can't decide not to pay that tenured faculty member just because you ran out of money. A slight motion attracted her attention and she looked down the dock toward the inside seating area of the restaurant. The sounds of Caribbean music drifted over from the restaurant at the next dock.

"We have the dock to ourselves," Beth said to Jonathan. "Our own private dock, our own musicians, food and drink brought to us by eager servants…" *Ça voulez vous encore*, she thought, thinking of her parents. Her mom used to call to her dad *"je t'aime. Je t'adore. Ça voulez vous encore?"* I love you. I adore you. How could you ask for more?

High school French, she realized now. Her parents had been children of the Depression. Worked after high school to support their extended families. Beth was their only child, born deliberately late, after the Second World War had ended and her parents had amassed a small nest egg.

Her father and mother had put themselves through college after they married – dad first, bachelor's degree, masters, PhD. Then her mother – bachelor's, master's, and still taking courses when breast cancer took her. By the time her mother died, Beth was old enough to see how hard they worked. Day jobs, night school; often each held two jobs. Dinner table conversations had taught Beth early that life was about education and hard work, and had left her with an abiding concern about security.

Only her mother had ever called Beth beautiful. Raw-boned, rather than slender, eyes too large, mouth too wide and too eager to spread into a broad grin exposing two chipped front teeth, dark brown hair now heavily mixed with grey, freckles, glasses. Crows' feet marked the corners of her eyes, and parallel parentheses encircled her mouth – the signs of a woman who smiled often and without care for wrinkles. She was in constant motion – either writing, or pacing, or gesturing with large, square hands, nails cut short. Tall, with broad shoulders and lean forearms with the muscles and veins clearly defined under the tan.

Where Beth was dark, Jonathan was fair. She was a whirling dervish, and he was the still calm center around which she moved. Right now, all her attention was focused on her salad, which she was trying to eat in as few bites as possible. Yet, slow and meticulous, Jonathan had already finished his salad. He put down his fork and looked at her.

"What have you been writing?" he asked.

"The names of the boats that go by, and the number and sort of people that are in them, the birds, and all that stuff. I want to remember. I wrote down some of the Japanese phrases from that old World War II phrase book I bought last night," she leafed back through the notebook, "like these: *Aranami*. That means rough waves. *Yatto desu* – all one can manage, what one can barely do. I like the way it sounds. It might come in handy some day. I might write some poetry using these phrases. Found poems; like found art, you know? Here's one I put together: *Ryoku-saki de/ Haru kara aki ni kakete/ Ippai ni*. It translates as: On one's journey/ from spring to autumn/ one's heart is too full."

"Nice."

"Nice, but, could I make a living at it? I don't think so. Writing medical pulp thrillers, maybe – mad scientist surgeon is secretly in league with the Mob; brave young, female, of course, intern turns him in, saves the day. But seriously, the translations are so quaint. *Furidasa* – to begin to rain. Not just to rain, but to begin to rain. So precise."

"Well, it better not *furidasa* tonight. We have a play to go to."

Crinkles appeared at the corners of his eyes, a small Jonathan smile, as he ate. He was one of those lucky individuals who only need glasses to read. He viewed the world through placid eyes that turned blue-grey in one light, flecked russet and gold in another. Here in the reflected glow of the setting sun, those flecks glistened like mica in granite. He had a legitimate reason to avoid the sun – his milky skin, prone to freckle, had already grown a few small basal cell carcinomas.

It was that sun sensitivity that led them to vacation, year after year, here in Woods Hole, where the library of the Marine Biological Laboratory provided a shady working space during the prime-UV hours. She had written many papers and several textbooks in that library. And Jonathan had written most of his research grant applications there. This year, she actually should be back at her job, at the collegiate research retreat that David, the Dean of the College of Medicine, had called on such short notice. Should have cancelled her vacation. Two years ago, she would have.

Just then, her salmon came, a nice piece glazed with Miso sauce and nestled on sticky rice. She hurriedly clipped her fountain pen to the inside back cover of her notebook and slipped it onto her lap to make room at the small table.

Jonathan ate precisely, scraping the sauce off the salmon and cutting the whole thing to equal-sized bits before eating. She used the side of her fork to cut big chunks, was half done before he even started. Surgeon's eating habits, Jonathan often called it. The food had to be shoveled in fast in case the OR, the ER, or the ICU paged.

When her salmon was gone, Beth sat up straight, took a deep breath, and looked at the ripples on Eel Pond where a large fish had jumped. She rubbed the thickened callus that partially encircled her right thumb. The callus was thickest on the inner aspect, just above the last joint, where the golden rings of a pair of scissors rested when she cut tissue, or suture, or the polyester mesh used to repair soft-tissue defects. Where the delicate rings of the elegant long handled needle holders sat as she manipulated a delicate half-circle needle through tissue, placing a stitch that might approximate the edges of a piece of bowel, two leaves of fascia, or close a hernia defect. Or a hemostat poised, jaws open, ready to control a spurting arteriole and stop the bleeding. The instrument always nestled comfortably against that ridge of callus, without riding up over the thumb. Sherlock Holmes would deduce that she was a surgeon. Who else would have this kind of callus? A seamstress, perhaps. Cutting lengths of cloth all day.

Jonathan looked up, saw her gaze out beyond the confines of Eel Pond and noted the slow rubbing of the callus. He waited, lips set in a firm line.

"I met with David last week," Beth said.

"You didn't tell me."

"Didn't want to talk about it." Reflexively, she leaned forward, lowered her voice even though they were alone at the dock and half a continent away from the hospital.

"Same issues?"

"The finances just get worse and worse. I'm doing more surgery than ever before, my whole department is, but the money just isn't coming in. We can't cover our expenses. It's not just my department, it's the whole college, but he seems fixated on surgery."

David had been an excellent surgeon before he made the move into administration. He had started out as a good dean, but he'd become increasingly focused on finances as the economy went sour. Even worse, he was now a surgical dilettante, cherry-picking the occasional easy case just to say he was a surgeon, and holding surgery to a higher standard than the other departments.

Maybe someone higher up was twisting his tail. The general decline in reimbursement for physician services coupled with a need to raise salaries to retain key faculty, had sucked David into a deficit financing mode for the whole College of Medicine. It wasn't sustainable. And surgery was supposed to be a cash cow, not a drain. It made you believe in academic tenure, which she bloody well had.

Tenure didn't, however, promise a good working environment. She was increasingly pulled in three directions. She sometimes joked that she spent 50 percent of her time taking care of patients, 50 percent of her time teaching and writing, and 50 percent of her time in meetings – and yes, that added up to more than 100 percent. There had to be an easier way to make a living. Why keep working? Take early retirement and finish that novel she'd been working on for the past five years. Or write poetry. Or go back to school. They'd get by on Jonathan's salary. But...she'd always assumed she'd work well into her 70's, like the surgeons who trained her. And she was only 59.

As she slid forward to the edge of her chair to tell Jonathan what David had said, she felt something slip. Heard a soft splash, such as a fish might make leaping out of the water. They both looked down. A purple-covered Buckthorne University notebook floated eight or ten feet below on the calm water. Her notebook.

The pocket in front held, among other things, an encrypted diskette full of departmental salary information. The pages were crammed with notes, observations, conversations. The past couple of days in Woods Hole. Notes about Coco, the harbor seal, whose companion Sandy had died of an ear infection in October, and how the volunteer who fed Coco every day had stayed with Coco all day for several days after that, but couldn't tell if Coco was grieving or not.

Notes about the 46 pilot whales that had stranded off the Northern coast of Cape Cod and were rescued, about the lighthouse and its fourth order Fresnel lens. Of clinics that had stretched from their norm of 25 to an unreasonable 50 when she filled in for another surgeon who had a heart attack. Poems she had written, the outline of a possible novel. Notes about patients and students. About a lawsuit filed by a disgruntled former employee. About the finances. About David. The notebook had been almost full.

The circular ripples were already fading away. None of the waiters had noticed. She wondered what they would do if she jumped in after it. The water probably wasn't very deep at this point. She felt a hot flush spread up from her chest.

"Do you write in permanent ink?"

"No, this ink washes away pretty easy. Let it go. I remember it all, anyhow. That's why I write it down, to remember it." Recalling the time she'd written in a light rain shower in Iceland, notes on how one could tell a glacial melt stream from an ordinary one. Those pages were blotted with white pox marks where each raindrop hit. Even a raindrop could efface the blue fountain pen ink she favored.

The notebook simultaneously swelled and sank lower as it became waterlogged, but stubbornly refused to sink.

"Let it go," she repeated softly, but they both watched it. Her name wasn't written on it. She never put her name on these notebooks, just in case she lost one somewhere around the hospital. When this one washed ashore in Martha's Vineyard, or Iceland, England, maybe Portugal, no one would know who wrote it. She had a sudden image of the notebook, a brave little sailboat, crossing the Atlantic Ocean, entering the Strait of Gibraltar, passing into the Mediterranean Sea, maybe the Adriatic.

The tide must have been going out. Ever so slowly the notebook floated across the small square of open water between their dock and the adjacent restaurant, toward the narrow channel that led under the drawbridge and out to Vineyard Sound. Why didn't it sink?

Causality, she thought, wondering for a moment why she couldn't reverse time, bring the notebook back onto her lap. Entropy is universal. The laws of thermodynamics are the law. If she only had a second chance – she'd put it away carefully this time. She'd tuck it into her bag and put the bag safely between her feet, plant one foot firmly on a strap for extra security.

They finished the meal in silence. Jonathan put on his reading glasses, added a generous tip to the credit card bill, and signed it. He carefully tore away the top and bottom blank parts of the customer's copy and placed the compact slip of paper into his wallet. They started up the hill.

As they came to the bridge they turned and looked back without even conferring with each other. Nothing. They crossed the bridge, and looked back from a better vantage point.

"There it is!" he pointed. About thirty feet away, a small purple rectangle floated slowly under the pilings that anchored the restaurants.

"All the times I've written on boats – on whale-watching cruises, even punting in Cambridge, remember? – nothing ever happened."

"Want to go after it?" He didn't sound enthusiastic. They had tickets to a play over in Dennisport. It began in just half an hour.

"Let it go," she said again, and they turned back up the hill together.

Later that night, after the play, the ice cream cones, and the hot bath, she nestled against Jonathan in the small motel room bed.

"The Marines," she said.

"What?"

"The US Marines don't leave their wounded behind enemy lines."

"You're muttering. Go to sleep," Jonathan said, as he turned toward her

* * *

Kento ga tsukanai/ Shimai niwa/ Sukitoru
I can't make out what it is/ finally, in the end/ becoming transparent.

The tide was low when they crossed the bridge into town the next morning. Pebbles and shells lay exposed under the Captain Kidd. Without discussing it, they stopped and peered under the shadows. Nothing. But it seemed to her, from looking at the terrain, that a small floating object might become trapped in the shallows under the pier rather than floating out to sea. Beth marched resolutely to the Food Buoy, where Jonathan bought the *New York Times*, *Wall Street Journal*, *Cape Cod Times*, and the *Boston Globe*. She picked out two muffins and fixed two cups of coffee to go.

They found a bench in the shade. Jonathan read the *NYT* and *WSJ*, while she checked the tide tables in the *Cape Cod Times*.

"I thought so. Low tide's in half an hour. I'm going after it," she said.

"Suit yourself," he replied. "Want me to go with you?"

"No, I'll be OK."

Jonathan nodded, and said, "Of course. I'll be in our usual spot."

She walked back to the bridge, taking with her a plastic grocery bag she'd tucked into her purse just in case. Choosing a moment when the bridge tender was looking out over Vineyard Sound, she slipped over the chain link fence and down onto the rocks. From there, it was an easy scramble down to the waters edge. No notebook in sight.

She bent over and ventured about six feet into the darkness under the restaurant. Low overhead. Pipes dripping, pilings black with seawater and some kind of organic slime. Barnacles. Periwinkles. Just as she was about to turn back, she glimpsed what looked like a piece of purple and white fabric. It lay deep under the restaurant, where the converging beach floor and ceiling of beams and pipes were only about three feet apart. She bent over farther and crept into the increasingly narrow space.

A small hermit crab scuttled away as she picked up the notebook. The sodden cover separated from the rest of the pages. Incredibly, the gilded clip was still in place. About six inches away, she saw the cap of the fountain pen. The rest of it was gone. She put the whole thing into her plastic grocery bag.

Getting back over the fence was not as hard as she had feared. A pipe jutting out from the Captain Kidd provided convenient leverage and Beth scrambled over easily. She walked up the hill to the motel, head high, carrying the plastic grocery bag.

On the balcony of their motel room, she carefully peeled each page back and interleafed the pages with blank paper from a spare notebook. It was tedious work in the sun. The paper had the consistency of wet toilet tissue. Some pages appeared completely blank, the ink completely gone, while others revealed ghostly writing. A few pages written in ballpoint pen were completely readable. She even found two almost completely dry pages in the middle of the book.

She straightened up and read, "... long clinic. We managed to finish by 5:30, then another hour to complete paperwork. David and I went over finances, which are in the tubes. Oh do I ever have the blues, so bad, so bad..." – that could have been any Monday from the past month or so. Aftermath of those meetings with David. I should just quit, she thought. Why go back to this?

She read on. "Yoder looks very weak. Needs blood..." – that had been a tough one. Chronically anticoagulated to prevent clotting on his artificial heart valve, Yoder had dropped his blood count on the fourth day after surgery – just when everyone thought he was past danger of bleeding. When she'd told him he would need another surgery to stop the bleeding, his reaction was simple – "Better get to it, doc." He and his wife had been told going into surgery there was a high risk, wasn't that why they had been sent to the University, after all? They accepted this just as they had faced good seasons and bad, times of too little rain, too much rain, or rain at the wrong time – good harvests and bad, high prices for corn and prices below cost of production. That calm confidence had transmitted itself to Beth, herself keyed up and edgy as any surgeon facing bleeding of unknown source. It steadied and calmed her, slowing her heart rate and breathing.

So that when Deirdre, a junior and relatively unseasoned resident, began obsessing – "what will we do if the bleeding is from... should we get him an ICU bed...what if he develops a coagulopathy?" as residents do, as she had been trained to do, Beth had said simply, "We deal with it step by step. First we find the bleeding site. We'll have to evacuate all the blood and clot and we'll be looking for that bright red trickle or stream and follow it backwards to the source. Once we find it, we hold pressure on it and then we obtain definitive control."

She said this, rather than the first thing that came to mind, which was, "don't even think that! Bite your tongue!" And so she transmitted Yoder's confidence and hers to Deirdre and even the Anesthesiology team, who got paid, after all, to worry about the patient and what the surgeons might do during surgery and how they could defend the patient.

Two weeks later, Yoder was ready to go home. Took her hand in his. That warm blunt hand, a couple of fingers missing from an old farm injury, "You take care of yourself, now, doc..." Wife quilting in the sunny chair by the window...

Beth sometimes thought that being a doctor was like spending your life on the road, traveling from one strange place to another. A long slow trip across a continent. You stop in a town, meet all sorts of interesting people, then you move on. The difference was that Beth stayed in one place, the hospital, and the interesting people came to her. People drifted in and out of her life.

She returned to the task of separating the wet pages. When she was satisfied, she put the whole thing into a Fed Ex box, left over from a set of galley proofs she'd received earlier that week. Put the whole thing under the leg of one of the wrought iron chairs to anchor it, and put a sign on it, just in case: "Please don't touch, papers drying".

* * *

Itsu shika/shikkari suru/hike o toronai
Without one's knowledge/to become steady, take courage/to yield to none

Jonathan was in their favorite spot, deep in the stacks of the MBL Library. He was carefully marking key phrases on a stack of reprints with a thin red ballpoint pen when she joined him. Not wanting to disturb the elderly scientist at the desk behind them, she gave him a broad grin, and a thumbs up sign. She whispered, "The Marines don't ever leave their wounded behind enemy lines. They'll shoot them instead."

"I don't think the Marines actually do that. The SEALS, maybe. But I know what you mean."

Passing behind him on her way to her usual writing space, she paused, caught both his shoulders with her hands and lightly planted a kiss between his shoulder blades.

The hell with David, she thought, as she pulled her own papers out of her knapsack and sat down to write.

PASSING STORM

I sat in our sunny library at home, leafing through the early retirement forms the dean had pressed into my hands at my last performance evaluation. Jonathan, my husband, has told me he will support whatever I decide to do. He's a cancer researcher. Spends his days in the lab. Issues are clear to him—experiments either work or they fail. Just like graduate students. Find the right gene, turn it off, and you just might cure cancer. I see things in shades of gray. I deal with uncertainty, with the human factor, with the limitations of medical knowledge. On the good days, he and I balance each other out.

One by one the dean had replaced my colleagues, other aging department Chairs, with younger and more malleable faculty. His own men, handpicked. Not a woman among the new crop, and I was in fact the only woman left among the old guard. I had been mulling over my options for a month now. Time was running out.

So I was lost in thought when a strange scuffling thud startled me. I looked over my left shoulder to see our aging cat,

Pumpernickel, standing beside me in a daze. She shook herself, turned, and walked slowly away. She must have attempted the leap onto the sunny window seat, an easy one for even a mature cat, but she had missed. She never missed. How old was she? Eighteen years? Nineteen? How old was she when we rescued her from the cold and the dark? Pitiful little wretch, shivering, coated with mud and fleas, her stomach bloated with worms. Couldn't have been more than a few months old. Old enough to be pregnant, it turned out. Not just worms in that belly. Oh well, how old do cats live anyhow?

I got up slowly and gently picked her up—placed her in the sun on the old Persian carpet that padded her favorite window seat. She just stood there, blinking in the sun, trying to gather her dignity, pretending she had jumped up there on her own as she had originally planned.

A few minutes later I went downstairs for a cup of tea and she followed. I watched her descend the stairs—carefully, step by step. Fully lowering herself onto one step—OK, that's done!—before tackling the next. Puppy-cat, I sometimes called her, because of her propensity to follow you from room to room. At night she slept outside the closed door of our bedroom, while Ninja, our young male shorthair, prowled the backyard. When I sat at my desk upstairs, Pumpernickel slept at my feet.

"Don't bother coming down," I told her. "I'm going right back upstairs." But she still followed me step by step. All I could do was hurry and get back before she got all the way downstairs.

When I returned a few minutes later, she was mercifully only halfway down the stairs. She stopped, blinked a couple of times, and slowly followed me back upstairs. When Pumpernickel was young, she had been a pencil-thief. It became a running joke—leave a pencil on a desk or table so that one end protruded slightly, and she would stand up on her hind legs, balance with her front paws, and delicately grasp the pencil in her teeth, pulling it forward until it fell off the table. At that point she would turn and walk away. Whatever interest had fueled the initial attack was spent, and she had no desire to continue the assault upon a fallen foe. Now, it was impossible to imagine that portly body stretching sufficiently to make the reach, or those short legs strong enough to provide the balance.

* * *

Two days later I was committed to give a talk to a group of high school kids in one of those innumerable small towns that dotted the area. A female role model. I had never felt less like one. Female failure, more like it. Jonathan came with me and drove. We'd gotten a quick early dinner at one of our favorite restaurants on the south side of town, and now we were on the back roads heading south.

Dusk was falling, and lights were starting to come on in houses. Here and there a red-tailed hawk sat high in a bare branch, looking for prey. I counted hawks for a while, then lost track in the deepening darkness. We passed occasional clusters of buildings—gas stations, repair shops, the "El Mariachi—authentic Mexican cuisine" restaurant. A tiny motel with two semis in the parking lot.

Jonathan drove with precision, hands at 10 and 2, keeping a steady pace designed to maximize fuel efficiency. A Beach Boys CD drummed in the background as the countryside rolled by. I recalled what one Midwesterner had told me when we first moved here: "So many people think the prairie is flat, but this part is still changing. It bears the shape of the geologic forces which shaped it."

Small farms, little towns—in the growing darkness, only scattered lights marked isolated farmhouses. The road narrowed, and oncoming headlights came with frightening regularity and delta-vee of 140 miles per hour, separated only by the double yellow lines.

"They just found another breast cancer gene," Jonathan announced. "It was written up in the *JNCI*—you really ought to read that journal," he added. "I got you that subscription last Christmas—do you ever look at it?"

Sure, between midnight and 1 a.m. when I have free time. In your dreams. I shifted uncomfortably in the passenger's seat and looked down. My feet hurt. I resisted the urge to put them up on the dashboard. Jonathan kept his car immaculate. Headlights seemed to come straight at us. "Watch it!"

"Relax, he was on his side of the line."

"I see these bozos all the time in the Trauma slot. They don't give a flip what side of the line they're on."

A comfortable darkness surrounded us. The music played on. *Let's go surfin' now, everybody's learnin' how, c'mon an' safari with me...*

"You need to keep up with these things," Jonathan persisted.

"I know, sweetie, I know. Tell me about this gene."

He launched into an enthusiastic technical description, which I followed for a few moments. My thoughts drifted. *If the deficit is $500,000 now, or closer to $750, it'll be over one million by the end of FY...damn it, the dean might be right.*

Jonathan fell silent.

"Sorry? I missed that last bit. Must have fallen asleep." I said softly, sitting up a bit straighter.

"Well, do you? I said, do you test all of your patients for these genes?"

"Get real. As if anyone would pay for it—and as if we knew what to do with the information. Most of the women I see with breast cancer don't have a family history," I said. I thought about clinic.

Janice, last Thursday. Tears seeping through clenched eyelids. Her husband, called in from work to provide support, reaching out his hand toward Janice, then clenching it in a fist. The usual beginning—we have a problem—then sliding gently into the fine-needle aspiration results—adenocarcinoma—from there into the diagnosis of breast cancer. And then Janice's anger and disbelief. But I had a normal mammogram three months ago. But no one in my family has ever had breast cancer. And finally—but I'm only 42!

The medical student passing the box of tissues we keep on the small desk in the consulting room. Nice business, when you have to keep a full box of tissues in every room. Silence. The room drawing in on itself, growing smaller. Going on with the explanation. Here's what we need to do…the classic strategy of cut/burn/poison. What had Janice done to deserve this? Janice's surgery—the cut—is tomorrow, 7:15 a.m., and even with the best timing it will be close to midnight before I get home to bed. I stifled a yawn.

"Then they don't eat right," Jonathan said.

"Come on, Jo, you know diet and exercise is just part of the picture." I reached over and turned up the volume as the Beach Boys crooned *She's real fine, my 409.* "Let's not quarrel. Cancer is cancer; all I know how to do is cut it out and hope for the best. Someone else in some lab somewhere, I hope, will finally solve the problem. Maybe you."

Jonathan rapped the steering wheel in time with the beat, and I drummed on the glove compartment in cadence, two aging baby boomers hurtling through the night. Signs indicated a curve to the left coming, and posted a 25 mph speed limit. I turned down the volume on the Beach Boys and cautioned Jonathan, "Careful. You really need to slow down here, this is a true right-angle curve." He slowed down a tad, then braked abruptly as the road seemed to end, only to resume off to the left.

"You weren't kidding! That's insane," Jonathan said.

Told you, I thought. *Males. They just don't listen. Don't slow down. Live hard and die young. Even Jonathan, careful and super cautious. Something changed when he got behind the wheel of a car. It brought out the primitive male instincts.* I said aloud, "The locals call it Carson's curve in honor of the first guy who flipped his car on that turn and survived. Hereabouts, they don't waste a single square foot of good farmland. I've flown over this part of the state in a small plane, visiting outlying clinics. From the air you can see how the roads are laid out in a grid. No fairing of the angles to accommodate speed. We get plenty of traumas off these roads, particularly in the winter."

We drove in respectful silence.

"There aren't any more of these, are there?"

"Not to my knowledge," I said, shifting to look out the window. I said abruptly, "Jo, I'm just getting so tired of it all. I'm really tired of telling women they have breast cancer and that all we can do is cut/poison/burn. I'm tired of the frigging administrators and I'm really tired of never having enough money to do the things we need to do in the department. I think I *will* retire."

"And do what?" There was a hint of alarm in his voice. I realized that he was probably afraid of all my nervous energy, with no focus. The house would explode. And then, too, there was my salary...

"I don't know. Write, maybe. Go back to school. Sleep, I think. Eat as much as I want whenever I want. Maybe I could work part time."

"You need to slow down. Take in a junior partner. Pass off some of the work to somebody else. You don't see the Chairman of Medicine down in clinic seeing patients, now do you? How many Chairs take trauma call, for instance?"

"Surgery's different. You can't lead a group of surgeons without operating. They won't respect you. You can't respect yourself."

"Or maybe just hand over the administrative load? What is it that you're tired of? Because if you're tired of the patients, if you're that burned out, you better get out. You're dangerous."

I shook my head. "Yeah, that would make the dean happy. That's just what he wants. It's not the patients, although, you know, this afternoon an old man told me he hated me. Came in septic, perforated diverticulitis, generalized peritonitis. We saved his life. Took out the bad colon, gave him a colostomy—it's only temporary, mind you, just until he gets over this. In a couple of months we can put him back together so he poops the natural way. And he's doing really well too.

"So today, on afternoon rounds, he says he hates me. And he means it. So I started to think about what I did to him. I cut him wide open, like a lobster, scooped out the bad part, stapled and sewed, and washed and cleaned, then brought out the end of his colon so he poops in a bag. Sewed him back together with big, wide stitches and finished the whole thing off with skin staples, wicks in between to prevent infection. Big tube down his nose to keep him from vomiting, another in his penis, IVs, no wonder he hates me."

"You saved his life, you said so yourself."

"Well, right now, he doesn't see it that way. And it seems like I don't even see it that way."

I turned up the Beach Boys again. *I get around, round, round, round, I get around...* Turned my face toward the dark passenger side window, away from Jo. Tried to think of something inspiring to tell the young students.

* * *

I was still edgy the next day when I walked into the OR. The room grew quiet as the anesthesiologist pushed drugs into Janice's IV. I held her hand, her fingers curled warm against mine. Two minutes later her eyelids closed, and her grasp relaxed. I pulled my hand away and undid the snaps at the top of gown, pulling it down to expose her breasts. There was little need for talk as we rapidly went through our preparations. The drapes went up, and we went to work.

The tumor lay deep in her right breast. But before we attacked it directly, we needed to harvest the sentinel lymph node—the guardian, in a sense, of her future. If that node turned out to be positive, we would be doing more radical surgery. And she would face more toxic chemotherapy and a more uncertain future.

I picked up the gamma probe and turned on the unit. Brought the probe near the incision, where the isotope had been injected. The unit began to squeal, becoming louder and higher pitched as I neared the injection site where the isotope remained concentrated, and fading as I drew back. Satisfied that it was working, I brought the probe over to the axilla and slowly moved the probe over the skin to find the hot spot over the node. The squeal waxed and waned. At the point where the noise was loudest, we made our incision.

I picked up the gamma probe, encased in a thin sterile polyethylene sleeve, and placed the tip in the wound. The squeal grew in intensity. Conversation fell silent. I moved the probe slightly until, satisfied that I knew where the node was, I handed it to the surgical resident.

"Here, you find it." We spread the tissues gently away from the region of interest.

"Look! There's a lymphatic!" An unnaturally intense azure-blue-tinged lymphatic vessel no thicker than a hair threaded through the buttery-yellow fat. We followed it to a fat blue lymph node. Gently teased it from surrounding tissues. Put the gamma probe on it. Hot, hotter than hell, off-the-screen hot.

"Got it! Count. Now."

"Fifty-two thirty-seven."

"That's a good one. Write it down. In vivo count, fifty-two thirty-seven."

We gently teased it out. I put a clamp across the tiny artery and vein entering through the base of the lymph node, and the resident cut the pedicle, releasing the node. Handed it to the scrub tech.

"Lymph node, sentinel. Send it to the lab, stat, touch preps. And warn the lab I'll be over shortly to look at the slides with them."

I lingered until the 4x4s returned pink, not red with blood, when removed from the newly saline-irrigated cavity. At that point I backed away from the table, peeling off gloves and stepping out of my gown.

"I'm going to the lab to check the touch prep," I announced to no one in particular. I wondered, briefly, who would be the faculty pathologist. Hoped it would be Greg, exceptional for speed, accuracy, and decisiveness. Once he'd taken a month off when his wife delivered prematurely, and there was a noticeable degradation in lab response time. Besides, his wife was a great cook, and she often sent him to work with a large cake pan full of baked goods to share.

There was a huddle of students and residents at the multi-headed microscope. I saw Greg's red hair, going in all directions as always, in the center of the group, and my stomach rumbled in anticipation of a treat. A resident was staining the touch preps of my lymph node as I entered. Greg wrapped up his assessment of the frozen section he was working on and picked up the phone. I heard his usual terse assessment. "George? On that kidney? You need to take more. Got tumor at the inferior resection margin. Give us another centimeter or so." He hung up the phone. "Hi, Beth. Sentinel node? They staining it for you? You want some banana bread, cream cheese icing? In the break room. Go get that node sliced," he added, scattering the students and residents. He lowered his voice and leaned forward, "They say you're retiring, Beth. Any truth to that?"

"Come to Path, have a snack, that's how we distract you from how long it's taking," added a resident as she ran my specimen through her processor.

"Don't believe everything you hear," I said to Greg and went for the goodies.

In the break room I wolfed down a large square of banana bread and was licking the last bits of icing from my fingers when Greg called, "Come and get it. Touch prep ready." His voice still had that touch of a Southern drawl. Reminded me of my years in Virginia. I felt the urge to lengthen my vowels, slow my speech.

Joining the group at the multiheaded microscope, I watched fields of lymphocytes speed by, intense blue, like fields of cornflowers crowded together, cytoplasm virtually nil. Here and there a larger cell, paler staining, a foamy macrophage, like chicory among the cornflowers. Or bachelor's buttons. They swept past faster than my eye could register. The taste of the cream cheese icing lingered on my lips. I thought of New Orleans—of strong chickoried coffee and begnets—as the fields of bachelor's buttons swept past. Greg scanned the field vertically, horizontally, systematically ensuring that no cell was overlooked. Finally he pushed back his chair. "Positive," he announced.

"Where?"

"There. And there. See those cells?"

I went back to the OR to do the additional surgery, and thought of what I would have to tell Janice when she woke up.

*　*　*

Janice was the last patient I saw on afternoon rounds that day. I told myself that I just wanted to give her plenty of time to emerge from anesthesia, but maybe I just dreaded telling her that her nodes were positive. When I knocked and entered her room, Janice was sitting upright in bed, wearing a soft, quilted bed jacket over her hospital gown. Her husband sprang to his feet from the chair on the far side of her bed.

In the postoperative waiting room, he had nodded gratefully—too choked up to speak—when I told him that I would explain the surgical findings to Janice. Now he stood bolt upright, lips compressed into a firm line.

I smiled at him and went and sat down on the foot of Janice's bed. Decades ago, one of my professors had taught me to do that, saying, "It puts you on the same level as your patients. They can look at you eye-to-eye. It makes you more human." Then he had winked and added, "Besides, it saves your feet."

I stalled for time by telling her where the incisions were. I took her through the surgery, step by step. Explained how I had looked at the cells under the microscope and there was no doubt, there was cancer. So I had taken additional lymph nodes…at that point I stood up and moved to her side, so that I could check her incisions and drain. Lifted up her soft, pink bed jacket, the lace crisp as only new lace, never worn or washed, feels. So that I would not need to look straight into those wide, brown eyes. No matter how many times you have to do this, it does not get any easier.

Her dressings looked fine, and I reassembled her coverings and sat down again.

"This means chemo, doesn't it?" she said.

"Yes, but you might have needed it in any event, because you are so young."

"I'll lose my hair."

"Yes, but it will grow back."

I answered several more questions, but the really big question—will I survive?—remained unasked and could not, in any case, have been answered. As I rose to leave, Janice asked one more question. "Is it true, Doctor, that you're leaving? That's what everybody says. Are you going to be around to take care of me?"

I sat back down again. *This must be what it feels like to explain to your small child that you are getting a divorce.*

I drew a slow, deep breath. "Janice, I'm going through a bit of a rough spot in my administrative capacity as Chair." I looked at her husband, a highly placed administrator in our public school system. He looked happy to finally be able to say something.

"Doctor, we understand that kind of thing. Janice stood by me when I had to deal with that age-discrimination suit a while back. It was thrown out but we spent many difficult hours agonizing over what it might do to my career, and by the time it was over I didn't even really want to continue as supervisor." He seemed to almost choke up again, and then continued, "Several folks spread rumors I was leaving. People kept asking me. I even caught one guy looking my office over, like he was planning to move in. Janice convinced me to stay on, and it's worked out, but we certainly understand that kind of stress." Janice nodded.

"I appreciate that. So, it is certainly true that I don't know what I am going to do. And rumors are flying. But I promise that

I will let you know if I decide to leave. And I'll make sure you are taken care of, if it comes to that."

"If it comes to that. Let's hope it doesn't."

I stood up, shook both of their hands, promised to look in early the next morning, and left.

* * *

That day ended unseasonably hot and humid. Heavy air lay on the lawn, and few birds sang. No stars were visible. I made one last attempt to call Ninja back inside from the back yard. No response.

Jo and I headed upstairs early, watched the weather report from bed. A cold front was predicted to move through the area. Strong storms, a possibility of tornadoes. Not unusual for that time of year. I looked up at the skylights over our bed.

"Maybe we ought to camp out downstairs tonight. They had hail the size of baseballs in Nebraska with that last storm," I said.

"It'll be OK. If there's a storm, we'll hear it, see the lightning; it'll be impossible to sleep through." Scientifically, objectively, rationally unconcerned as always. *He's my rock*, I thought. *How am I going to tell him I've decided to quit? He expects me to stand and fight. Stand up to the dean, the entire university. How do I tell him there's no fight left?* Now he reached over and turned out the light, held me close, stroked my hair.

* * *

I awoke in total darkness, completely disoriented. Something heavy was on my chest, moving on top of me. It was Pumpernickel. How had she gotten up there? I picked her up and put her down on the rug. She made a soft growling sound, deep in her throat.

The dark was unnatural, I realized, searching for the small lights that defined our bedroom—the alarm clock on my side of the bed, the tiny monitor lights on the smoke alarm and carbon monoxide detector, the clock radio on Jonathan's side. Power failure. Wind buffeted the loose screens on the back deck, went keening through the slotted covers of the eaves. Jonathan didn't stir. He had run a 10K race earlier that morning, and now, atypically, he slept like a stone.

I got up, put on my glasses and robe, and went downstairs by feel. Stood at the window in the stairwell and looked out, feeling Pumpernickel press against my right leg. I could barely distinguish the tree line as a surging bulk of black on dark, greenish-gray. The light was mottled, changing from moment to moment. A full moon, behind rapidly shifting clouds. A high-pitched howling came from the northwest corner of the house as the wind, intensifying, fluted through the eaves.

I went to the back deck and opened the door, the wind pushing the door in against me as soon as I unlocked it. I stepped outside to call Ninja. Wind-chimes clamored from the back deck, barely audible over the wind. Ninja came immediately, running low and fast as close to the house as possible and into the door. My eyes had adapted to the scant, strange light. He looked unnaturally large. I reached down and touched him— full piloerection. "Settle down, settle down," I said. He made a faint plaintive sound deep in his throat.

I ran up the stairs and shook Jonathan awake. "Storm, almost here. Feels like a big one. Power's out. Let's go downstairs."

Jonathan lifted the Venetian blinds on the bedroom window, looked outside for a long moment. I stood by his side, with Ninja and Pumpernickel pressed against me. Jo turned and picked up a flashlight from his bedside table, thumbed it on.

"Let's go," he said.

We gathered up pillows and a quilt and went down into the basement spare room we had fitted as a guest bedroom. Our house, bought because it was airy and light, now seemed ominous. Too many windows. Too much glass. Too many skylights. Even this room, our made-do storm cellar, had a small window, although it was shielded by the back deck and the pyracantha bushes. Even more important, the window looked east, away from the prevailing winds and weather. There was a small bathroom adjacent, and we could go in there, hide in the bathtub under a mattress, the ultimate tornado shelter of last resort.

I looked out the small window. Total darkness. The pyracantha bushes, planted fifteen years ago and now a large thicket, totally screened our view.

"Stay away from the window," Jonathan said. I pulled back. Jonathan stood the flashlight on end on a small table so that the beam illuminated the ceiling and thus, indirectly, the rest of the room. To my dark-adapted eyes, it was a welcome sufficiency of light. He pulled down the Venetian blinds and closed the curtains. He had taken out candles, matches, another flashlight, the small battery-powered radio we kept down there.

He struck a match, lit a candle in the small, festive holder my mother had given us one long-ago Christmas. He carefully centered the painted glass chimney, fitting it into place on the holder so as to contain the flame and protect it. Scenes of a New England Christmas flickered and cast shadows on the walls. He turned off the flashlight to conserve the battery.

We sat on the edge of the bed, close to the puddle of warm light. The room was small and snug with the door closed. I lifted Pumpernickel up onto the bed, and Ninja jumped up beside us. I pulled the quilt over both of us and around the cats while Jonathan tried to tune the radio to our local station. Nothing but static. I stroked Pumpernickel. Felt her begin to purr.

"You're a smart old cat, aren't you? A good old smart old cat." I turned to Jonathan and said, "What time is it?"

Jonathan looked at his watch. "It's just 3:00 a.m."

"Could be a long night. We should get some sleep. Safe enough down here." Neither of us moved. Jonathan fiddled with the dials on the radio, extended the antenna to its full stretch, coaxed a faint signal into semiclarity. A Chicago station. Something about strong storms across the upper Midwest. Multiple tornadoes sighted on Doppler radar, impossible to estimate damage at this time.

Even here, deep in the basement, we could hear the wind striking a rising and falling note through the eaves. At times, the house seemed to shake.

In the hospital, I knew, the nurses would have moved all the patients into the central core, beds and all, away from the big glass windows. In the sub-basement the emergency generators, eight of them, each as big as a school bus, would be thrumming. There was enough diesel fuel in the tanks to last a week.

I wondered who was on call. Whoever it was, they would need to cope with whatever happened. Nothing would be on the road this night.

I leaned against Jonathan. His arm encircled my back. "Did you mail that application for early retirement yet?"

"Not yet. I'm having second thoughts."

I felt him relax slightly. He took a deep breath and said, "Then take sabbatical leave."

I shook my head and said, "I thought about it. Won't work. Taking a year off sounds fine, but how would I come back? If they learn to get along without me, how would I fit in again?"

"You could take less than a year. Six months, maybe just three or four."

"Long enough to lose my edge. To lose my patients." I shifted under the quilt, leaned back on some pillows. "I could step down as Chair, let them recruit some young hotshot, but stay active as a surgeon. You know, things are getting better. Financial deficit's actually getting smaller, we filled in the Match, things are improving, it's a good note to end on. I hate to quit now, when it's getting better. But, you know, I could step down, I could just teach and operate. I'm a good teacher, I love to teach, and I'm a good surgeon. A couple more years, or not—will it matter a thousand years from now? Even five years from now?"

"Who cares?"

"And I keep thinking about the moon, how long ago those craters formed, and how if we didn't have the moon to stabilize our orbit, there might not even be life here. But it doesn't just do that, it lights our sky by night. And it's just the perfect visual size to produce solar eclipses from time to time. What are the odds of that? If ice, the solid form of water, didn't float instead of sinking like just about every other compound does, we wouldn't exist. Water would be locked into ice forever. Frozen like Mars. Lifeless."

"So...what is your point?"

"So, I don't know. Somehow it seems selfish and indulgent to opt out. A big part of the art of being a surgeon is just being there for your patients; you drain pus, stop bleeding, remove things that have gone bad. Rotten appendixes, bad gallbladders, breast cancers. Stuff like that. Be strong for them. It's work of my hands. It's even left its mark on my body.

"I sweat in the OR, I get tired, I get angry, I get tendinitis, but most of the time, I seem to help people. By cutting them open. It's a really primitive way to earn a living, but I'm pretty good at it. I've spent enough time learning how." I rubbed the callus on my right thumb. My wedding band glowed dully in the candlelight.

Jonathan remained silent, and in his silence the moaning of the wind around the house grew louder. The candle flame wavered as the house shook. Something shattered upstairs, a window or a skylight. Jonathan held me tighter.

I went on, "Surgery is what I do, it's what I am. It's too late to change."

"You can do both. I think you know the answer. Let someone else take over the administrative burden. Step down as Chair. Keep what you like to do. Operate. See patients. Work with the students."

"Maybe." I thought about one of my junior faculty members—heavily recruited to a better job in LA, and how good it felt when he decided to stay. I thought about the promises I had made to the new residents, and my patients, promises to be there for them in the years to come. I thought again of the lines of the poem, *"But I have promises to keep, and miles to go before I sleep…"* It seemed that the wind slackened a bit, only to howl with renewed strength a few minutes later. Something heavy crashed down outside the window. I snuggled closer to Jonathan.

Sometime later we must have fallen asleep. The candle had burned down and guttered out in a pool of wax, and when Jonathan lifted the blinds, there was sunlight outside.

* * *

Later that morning I sat at my childhood desk and looked at the retirement forms one last time. Everything was there— the necessary enclosures, all questions answered—I scanned the forms through and then slowly and deliberately tore the forms in half lengthwise once, then again, and again, until the bundle was too thick to tear. I put the pieces into the wastebasket.

Sun poured through the library window, illuminating the slightly moth-eaten fur of Pumpernickel and adding russet highlights to Ninja's sleek coat as they lay sleeping, curled against each other. Branches were down in our back yard. The skylights had broken over our bed, leaving the bedroom sodden and glass-strewn. It would be a while before we could sleep there. I drained the last of my coffee and stood up, ready to go make rounds. To speak with Janice and her husband. And then to begin the clean-up work, to move some of our things to the spare bedroom, to adapt.

TRAUMA SERVICE

Beth swam desperately through the cold, dark water of Eel Pond, evading jellyfish the size of bicycle tires. Just as she reached the Woods Hole dock, the insistent chirping of her pager awakened her.

She extended her right arm to reach for the phone on her bedside table, and encountered empty space. Opening both eyes, she remembered that she was in the Trauma Call Room. It was 3 a.m., the hour of the wolf. Beth opened one eye, checked the number. The Burn Unit.

She rolled over to her left. The call room was so small that the tiny bunk bed was shoved up against a window that over-looked the helipad. The floodlights were on, and she could see the orange windsock standing out half-extended in the wind. *There must be a chopper coming in.*

"Sorry to wake you up, Dr. Abernathy, are you on call for burns?"

She recognized the voice and the halting, tentative tone. Bob Huber, the resident assigned to the Burn Unit, was still a bit nervous about calling up senior attending surgeons in the middle of the night. "Yes, I'm it. What have you got?"

"One, maybe two patients. Coming from Webster City. A house fire. There's an infant, about two years old, sixty percent body surface area burns. There's also an adult male, but we don't know if we'll get him yet. He's not badly burned." Bob went on to detail the distribution of burn injuries on the baby – both hands, both arms, torso, both legs.

Sounds like more than sixty percent she thought sleepily, running the burn chart in her mind, toting up percentages by the rule of nines. *Nine percent for the front of the baby's head, nine percent for the back of the head, eighteen percent for both arms, eighteen percent for the front of the trunk and eighteen percent for the back, and we're up to…* but she had lost track. *We'll see soon enough.*

Bob was winding down his account. "I told them to intubate the baby and start an IV with Ringers solution. I accepted both of them, if they want to send both. The man may go to Lutheran."

"How far away is Webster City?" *Should I go back to sleep, or get up now and get a cup of coffee?*

"They're about fifteen minutes by chopper. MedEvac is on the way."

Coffee, then. But she fell back against the pillow in the dark. *I'll just drowse a little. If I don't let myself fall deeply asleep, I'll hear MedEvac coming in for a landing. How convenient, right outside my window.* But she did fall deeply asleep and the pager went off again. Rolled out of bed, no time for coffee, just a splash of water on her face and a quick brush of the teeth, an Advil for the headache already throbbing even though the day hadn't really started yet. Up the single flight of stairs to the Burn Unit, one step at a time, to get the blood pumping.

* * *

The admissions bay in the Burn Unit was brightly lit and crowded. The helicopter nursing crew lingered outside, gathering up their gear and cadging coffee from the night ward clerk. Probably recounting what they found at the scene. Very likely one of them had done the intubation and started the IV – they were better at it than some docs.

"What happened?"

"House fire. Boyfriend was supposed to be watching the baby, fell asleep smoking on a couch. Baby's two years old, male. Starting to make some urine, I think."

"Good job." Urine was good. If the kidneys were getting blood enough to make urine, the rest of the body, including the brain, was probably doing all right. She signed the papers, accepting the burden. The baby was swaddled in layers of transparent plastic film. His skin was sooty.

The medical student on call that night was a slender young Korean-American woman named Jenny Kim. "Why is the baby wrapped in plastic?" she asked. It wasn't in their textbook.

"It's standard household plastic wrap, just like you use in your kitchen. Our Burn Unit Director, Dr. Gilbert, has taught all the rural hospitals and ambulance crews to stock it. It's cheap, clean, and effective. These patients used to come in wrapped in wet sheets. They'd arrive colder than a dead mackerel, even in August, and we'd spend most of the night trying to warm them up." She smiled. You could track the geographic extent of Gilbert's outreach efforts by whether or not the patient arrived wrapped in plastic. Obviously he'd made it to Webster City.

Her duty was simply to shepherd this tiny patient until Gilbert came in to make morning rounds. He'd come in now, if she called him, but he needed his sleep too, and she'd seen plenty of these herself. *Too many. Does the company know what we use their plastic wrap for?* she wondered. *Is it Dow Chemical? Didn't they bring us napalm?*

Gilbert spent part of the Viet Nam war years fulfilling his military obligation in Antarctica. "No ma'am, the Midwest winters really didn't bother me very much," he'd said. "Yes ma'am, you really can hear the Aurora. No, ma'am, it's not inside your head, it's outside, it's a real sound." Talked about getting lost in a blizzard once. He and his men did what they'd been told, linked arms to form a human chain and walked in what they thought was the right direction. Came to base. "We were lucky," he said.

Somehow Gilbert was always "lucky" and his patients always did well. All the burn nurses carried his home phone number in their wallets in case one of their own kids got hurt. *He's made this Burn Unit one of the best in the country.* She suppressed the urge to call him. She knew what needed to be done.

The burn nurses swarmed over the baby. Beth stood in her favorite spot at the foot of the gurney, where she could see everything. Jenny stood slightly behind her. Bob hovered uncertainly off to the left, following directions from June, the most experienced burn nurse of the team.

Good, Beth thought. *He knows when to listen.* The respiratory therapist was adjusting the ventilator – the pulse oximeter read 95%, not bad, but not perfect either. There was a small amount of dark urine in the pouch, the heart rate read 190 – *what's normal for a two-year-old? There is the peds resident, ask her...*

The burns were bad. She could see that. The heat of the burn had cooked the skin, turning it into tough, dry leather. She could see thrombosed veins through the translucent eschar in places, the skin on an overcooked turkey drumstick. Full thickness injury, the skin completely destroyed.

She turned her attention to the team. Bob had settled into a familiar routine, punching the numbers into the calculator fastened to the wall, entering data in the proper order to calculate the baby's fluid requirements. Gilbert had had this particular resident on the burn rotation for just two weeks, but his teaching had been thorough. Beth checked the MedEvac charts – total fluids, intake and output – Bob would need that information next.

Truth was, this well-oiled machine that Gilbert had built here on the eighth floor of the hospital hardly seemed to need her. Safety lay in routine and they all knew the drill. She thought wistfully of the dark call room and the warm bed.

June looked up. "Beth, I can't Dopple any pulses in either hand." *Might have known.* The burned skin of the child's arms and hands was cutting off circulation as the underlying tissues swelled in response to massive injury. It was as if the baby wore elbow-length inelastic gloves that were several sizes too tight.

Beth looked at the little fingers, so cunningly made. Each tiny finger was pulled into that claw shape she'd come to associate with the need for an escharotomy. *Those weird concavities between the knuckles, where the skin is drawn so tight it has actually pulled in. I'm going to have to cut those tiny fingers to save them.*

"Let me try." Maybe the nurse was inept – *June? The best nurse they had?* – or maybe the fingers were too tiny, the settings on the machine were wrong, or the battery was dead. She tried the probe on her own wrist. "Whish-a-whish, whish-a-whish!" the triphasic signature of her own pulse, fast and hyperdynamic from stress. *Easy, old girl. A couple of deep breaths. Slow the heart rate, you're going to need steady hands.*

She tried it on the tiny groin and found the femoral artery – a loud, fast, clear signal – then tried the brachial artery on the inside of the elbow. Found it. Moved down to the wrist. *Nada.* Tried both sides. No radial artery, no ulnar artery, nothing. Tried the palmar arch and the digital arteries on each side of the fingers. *Stupid. If the radial and ulnar are blocked, nothing will reach the hand.* But she knew that she desperately wanted not to have to cut those tiny fingers. Hands got to her. They always had. *And this one's only two years old.*

She turned to Bob and asked him, "Have you ever done an escharotomy?"

He shook his head. "No".

Well, then, you'll learn. She straightened up and "We'll need iodine, number ten blades, sterile gloves, gowns, masks, lots of bandages, and have a cautery in case we need it." June was already assembling the items. She knew the drill. "How's his blood pressure? Can we give him some morphine?"

That was silly. Skin that badly burned had no functioning pain receptors. That was one of the tests for a third-degree burn. But this would be bad enough for all concerned with that gesture. "Morphine all around," she wanted to say. *Not funny.*

Beth retreated to the back room while they got ready. Privilege of rank. Coffee. A few swallows, just enough, the mud in the bottom of the pot at this hour would make your hands shake for sure. Distracted herself by explaining to Jenny, "We're going to do an escharotomy. 'Eshar' is a thick layer of dead skin. '-Otomy' is a suffix that means to cut or incise. So escharotomy means to cut or incise the eschar."

"Beth, we're ready," June called. All too soon. She walked back in briskly, put on a mask and gloves, and scrubbed her hands at the sink.

"Bob, I want you to watch carefully. I'll do one side, then you will do the other." Taking the #10 scalpel blade naked, without a handle, so as to control it even more precisely, she gripped it close to the tip of the blade, her own gloved fingers shielding most of it so just the very point protruded. She showed Bob how this helped limit the depth of the cut.

"Be very careful. It's easy to cut yourself. And very easy to cut too deep. You need to cut just deep enough to get it to separate. Watch." She drew a delicate straight line down the inner aspect of the sooty left forearm from elbow to wrist, using just the tip of the blade; like drawing a line with a fine-tipped pen.

The eschar sprang apart to expose buttery, yellow fat, confirming the need for the procedure. She repeated the process on the opposite side of the arm. The eschar spread open as if she had split the seams of a too-tight sleeve. The edges began to bleed, as capillaries reacted to the release of pressure.

"Post-ischemic hyperemia," Beth commented. She showed Bob and Jenny that the eschar was now loose, and then swiftly wrapped the forearm in dry gauze. "Jenny, I need you to hold pressure on this while I work on the hand. That will limit blood loss. A baby this size doesn't have much to spare."

She cut down each side of the hand and began on the fingers. The lines were very similar to the seams on a cheap pair of gloves. *Careful. Careful. Too deep, and tendons, nerves, or arteries could be damaged. Keep to the recommended lines, which should put you in a safe region. This tiny hand should be gripping a teddy bear. This baby should be safe in bed at home.*

She knew that it had to be done, that these cuts would preserve the function of the hand, not harm it, but she felt herself going remote, behind some crystalline shell. *Cut down both sides of each finger, that's ten cuts on each hand, and extend the cuts onto the palm and back of the hand to release the intrinsic muscles. Has to be done. Each cut must be done, and must be done right.*

Sweat beaded Jenny's face, but she was still gamely holding on. June shoved a chair under the student from behind and Jenny sat down heavily, without losing her grip. June wrapped the hand and shifted Jenny's hands so that one hand compressed the forearm, the second compressed the hand.

"Hold it up, if you can. It will bleed less. We may need the cautery, but it's easy to burn too deep and cause additional damage. Most of this should stop with pressure."

She straightened up. *My back. Don't bend over.* But there was no helping it. Wiped her forehead with the shoulder of her gown so the sweat wouldn't drip on the baby. The younger burn nurse was sitting off in a corner, head between her knees. Bob looked like he didn't want any part of this. His own child was about a year old now – she recalled the plump, gurgling babe in arms Bob's young wife had toted to the annual picnic. The baby's heart rate was steady in her ears, the cadence of the beep-beep-beep of the monitor a reassuring rhythm.

"I'll do the other side if you like. You will be doing these yourself soon enough." He nodded, relieved. She was relieved too, truth be told. This was no job for a neophyte. *Why the bloody hell did that man smoke in bed? Don't they ever learn? But, as Gilbert says, there's no end to the supply of burn bozos.*

They were done soon enough. Beth cleaned the sweat off her face, washed her hands, and headed out to the waiting room. Stopped on the threshold and looked for the family. Inside, a group of about 10 casually-dressed people laughed, drank pop, talked on cell phones. A murderous rage built inside her. She backed out of the room. Pulled the young burn nurse, now recovered from her queasiness, to her side.

"You come with me. Your job is to keep me from killing those people."

With the nurse by her side, Beth marched back into the waiting room. "I'm Dr. Abernathy. Who are the parents?"

The teenaged girl wearing a cropped tank top that revealed a tattooed midsection paused her phone conversation and gum-chewing long enough to say, "I am," and then put the cell phone back to her ear. The room fell silent.

An older man came up behind the girl, took the phone out of her hand. "Tanya, I'll take care of it," he said to the girl. "She'll call you back," he said into the phone, punched a button, clapped the phone shut, and dropped it into the pocket of his jacket. A baby crawled toward Beth, pacifier in its mouth. Looked up at Beth. Opened its mouth, dropped the pacifier, and began to cry.

The young nurse reached down and lifted the baby up into her arms. It wailed. In the corner of the room, three sullen-looking adolescent males huddled.

"How's he doing?" asked the older man. "I'm his granddad."

"He's alive," Beth said evenly. "He's very badly burned. He may lose the use of his hands. And he's going to need a lot of surgery." She went on to describe the extent of the burns.

"But he's going to be OK, isn't he?" Tanya finally asked.

"Depends upon your viewpoint. He should survive this injury. We'll do everything we can to ensure that, and to minimize scarring. Babies have very tender skin. His burns were so deep they cut off the circulation to his fingers. I had to make cuts…"

"You cut him? You *cut* his hands?"

"We had consent from your mom. She was the only person we could reach, and it couldn't wait." She went on to explain what had been done and why, ending with, "The burned skin is dead. We cut through dead tissue. All that dead tissue will be cut away and he will need skin grafts."

Tanya popped her chewing gum and said, "When can I see him?"

"Very soon. They're putting him in a crib now."

"I have to go see Bret. He got burned too. They took him to Lutheran."

Beth folded her arms across her chest, drew in a deep breath, and held her tongue. Waited.

Tanya suddenly looked very young. "Sam," she said. "My baby's name is Sam."

* * *

Three weeks later, Beth was finishing afternoon rounds alone. She paused at the door of the solarium just off the nurse's station in the Burn Unit. A chubby male infant gurgled and babbled in a playpen. Someone had draped a spare stethoscope around the baby's neck, and he had a surgeon's cap a bit askew on his head. The baby's arms and legs, even his hands and fingers, were swaddled in white gauze, but the tips of his fingers were free. The pads of his fingertips looked red, swollen, tender. The infant looked up at Beth and kicked a small stuffed animal in her direction. He began to cry. It was Sam, she realized.

Beth stepped up to the playpen, knelt down, and picked up the toy. Sam reached out toward her and she tilted her head back to look carefully at his hands through the bottom half of her lineless bifocals. Peeled back the edge of one gauze from the tip of a tiny thumb to expose a cleanly healing skin graft. Counted the fingers. All ten were still there. She held out the toy. Sam smiled, reached out, and tried to grab it.

PREDATORS

Beth awoke around two a.m. to the ululating howling of coyotes. A full moon shone through the skylight. The coyotes sounded very near. Their calls went from one individual to another, cascading, escalating and then falling apart into a chorus of yips. These sounds had not been part of her East coast megalopolis upbringing, but were common here in the suburban Midwest. Like tornadoes, another thing she had learned to live with. Beth shuddered in the sudden silence, and nestled closer to her husband. Slept.

* * *

Twenty-four hours later, well into her on-call stint at the hospital, Beth took a seat on an empty gurney, positioning herself so she could see directly down to the ambulance bay doors, and waited for the next trauma to arrive. It was said to be a hunting accident, although what this guy was hunting late at night in mid-winter was unclear. Shotgun blast to the abdomen, eviscerated. The chief resident sat down a respectful six inches away.

"Bet you saw a lot of this at Bellevue," he said wistfully.

"Not shotguns, but certainly lots of penetrating trauma...we did have a busy trauma service." She chuckled, shook her head, and continued, "You know, when I was there, they brought in this new guy to run the emergency room, and he set up all these protocols..."

"Research protocols?"

"Some. Mostly they were just protocols to tell you what labs you could order. To cut down on waste and inefficiency, maybe improve patient care. His name was Nelson, and he had this big thick red pen and he'd come in the next morning and go through the charts from the night before and write "WTF" in big red letters all over the order sheet if someone had ordered something he didn't agree with...right on the chart, WTF, WTF."

"WTF?"

"Stood for - What the fuck? So, that's what we all called him - WTF - he died of an MI, right there in his office. Was going through a chart where someone had ordered a troponin level on a patient who was hypotensive after a stab wound, wanting to rule out an MI, and old Nelson just started yelling "WTF! WTF! Doesn't anyone know how to treat hypovolemic shock?" and keeled right over. Say, I thought somebody told me you were a former SEAL. Didn't you see any trauma?"

"I wasn't a SEAL, Dr Abernathy, but I worked with SEALS. I trained as a combat medic. They had us doing these simulated exercises off the west coast – we'd be trying to start IV's on each other, all hypothermic, in wet suits, nighttime, heavy surf, guys firing over your head simulated rounds... gets a bit old. Weapons aren't designed to kill any more; they're designed to maim. That way you take three guys out with one shot – two guys taking care of their buddy so he doesn't exsanguinate. I never saw combat. One time – you know, they have these little submarines, they call them SEAL Delivery Vehicles, about the size of a VW bus and they just stuff the SEALS into them and off they go. Well there was this guy, kept puking. Just kept puking and puking, and I couldn't feel a pulse, tossing around in that little sub. He made it through to the end of the exercise but he lost 10 pounds, puke and sweat. I dunno how much I lost..." he stopped talking, realizing that Beth had stopped listening.

They both stood up suddenly, just as the big double doors at the end of the long hallway opened. Two dark navy jumpsuited young women came barreling down the hall toward the trauma room, propelling a gurney with what looked like a huge bright orange quilted burrito on it. IV bags hanging. Their patient.

Beth watched them pass and thought about her husband, Jonathan, wrapped up warm in bed, under their big down comforter. Wondered if the coyotes were howling. She pushed that thought firmly out of her head and stood for a few moments, letting them get the patient into the crowded trauma bay. Saving her energy for the OR, when it would be needed.

She elbowed her way to the side of the patient and opened the quilted burrito wrap. Inside the burrito was a scrawny little guy, mid-thirties, with a couple of tattoos. Hunter, or hunted? Large white gauze dressings covered his belly, and a ribbon of blood snaked down his flank. She lifted one corner of the dressing, just enough to peek underneath. About four loops of small intestine, dusky and purple in color, lay out on his abdominal wall. One loop had a hole blasted right through it, she noted. Succus, iodine, and blood combined in small streams along his flanks and puddled on the side of the gurney. She replaced the dressing.

"Yup. Eviscerated. Needs to go the OR. I want a chest x-ray, abdomen, and I want blood ready and I want him in the OR in ten minutes. What do we have for access?"

The chief resident was already busy getting a large bore IV line into the patient's inner elbow, the tender area where the big veins were close to the surface.

"We need to get him unwrapped and check him over quick before we go up. Check his back. Might be more than one hole in this guy. Ten minutes, no more. What's his BP?"

"90 over palp."

"Let's move it, people. Hang a unit of O-neg."

* * *

In less than fifteen minutes, the team unloaded him onto the OR table in good old OR #3, the biggest OR, where the blood warmer and rapid infuser, and all the trauma stuff stood ready. Kim Sook, the anesthesiologist, was an older man, steady and fast. His formal precision of language dated back to his under-graduate days at Oxford, but he had done his residency at one of the big inner city hospitals of the US, where trauma was a constant companion.

Beth barely had time to check the labs and x-rays on the computer screen before Dr Kim said softly, "You may cut when ready, Dr Abernathy." He made an expansive gesture with his left hand toward the belly of the patient. His right hand moved busily across the anesthesia record, making little marks for pulse, blood pressure, and respiration. The circulating nurse drew in her breath sharply, a little "huh" sound, when Beth peeled off the dressings and exposed the bowel.

"Uh, how do you want me to prep?" the nurse finally said.

"Just pour it over the whole belly, bowel and all, Iodine. We'll drape wide in case we need a vein patch or something. Both groins, lower chest."

Another nurse burst into the operating room, arms laden with blood bags. "Here's your blood," she said to no one in particular, and started putting the units into the OR refrigerator.

"I'll take that, if you don't mind," said Kim, holding out his hand. He reached up and took down a flaccid empty blood bag and replaced it with a fat new one, opened the IV drip regulator wide open. He had the rapid infusor up and running, so that the blood would be warmed as it went into the patient's veins, and it would pump in a liter in just over a minute if you wanted it to. The blood was flowing at a moderate rate, but he was obviously ready to dial it all the way up if he had to.

The scrub nurse had draped the patient with sterile green towels and sheets, and now all that was visible was a squared-off omega-shaped expanse of flesh, with the eviscerated bowel at the center. Beth took her place on one side, and motioned for the medical student to come stand beside her. The scrub nurse and the chief resident stood opposite.

"We're starting," the chief resident said, and made an incision from just under the breast bone to the upper aspect of the hole through which bowel protruded. Beth held the bowel back with her hands, placing a malleable ribbon retractor between the bowel and the skin so that he could cut without fear of injuring the bowel. He followed a similar process at the bottom, making the incision from the eviscerated area down to the pubic bone, so that when the incision was opened, the entire abdomen opened up like a book.

They quickly put Babcock clamps across the two holes in the damaged bowel, and Beth gave the eviscerated loops to the medical student to hold. "Here, take these," she said. The intestines had already started to feel cold. Dying by inches, this man was. Blood poured over the edges of the incisions, dark, partially congealed. "Old blood," she said. "Couple of liters." Kim nodded and watched closely.

They rapidly packed the abdomen off in quadrants, using clean white cotton pads to contain and isolate the areas. There was fresh bleeding from the root of the mesentery of the small bowel, an evil place to get hemostasis. Take a stitch a bit too deep, and you might permanently damage the blood supply to the entire intestine. Beth pinched the bleeding area off with thumb and forefinger, temporizing while they looked for any additional damage.

"Found the bleeder. Now we need to find the wadding," she said. And, out of long-standing habit, started talking to the medical student just to compose her thoughts, slow her pulse rate, prepare for the next phase when they would have to find and repair all the injuries, carefully get meticulous hemostasis.

"Do you understand how shotgun shells work?" she asked him. He shook his head no. "Well, it's something like this. The shot is propelled out of the gun. The diameter of the shell corresponds to the diameter of the gunbarrel, and that is the gauge of the shotgun, you see. The shell looks like a hollow cylinder. Often it's made of lightweight plastic. Inside the cylinder, it has a small charge and a lot of small pellets. The size of the pellets differentiates birdshot, which is small, from buckshot, which is large. This guy looks like he was shot with birdshot, because the pellets we found in his clothing were tiny – remember? Lucky for him." The student nodded.

"Well, inside the cylinder with the pellets there is a small charge to disperse the pellets and this charge ignites just after the shot leaves the gun. You can tell how far someone was from the gun by the scatter pattern. He was shot almost point blank, because the hole is small. Even though the pellets were small, the aggregate mass plus the exploding charge blew this hole in his belly. You see, the hole in his belly was almost big enough for me to stick my fist into, if it hadn't been full of his guts. So the shotgun casing and wadding, which holds it all together, is probably inside him somewhere, and we have to get it out. It's a foreign body, potential source of infection, plus the sheriff will want it for evidence."

Meanwhile, they were moving rapidly throughout his abdomen, scooping up clots of blood and tossing them into a waiting basin, looking for fresh bleeding, searching for holes.

"I've got it!" the resident yelped, holding out a twisted plastic cylinder.

"Good work," Beth said. "Now, where's the wadding? It ought to be nearby."

They were still searching, feeling and looking between coils of bowel, still cool to the touch from shock, down in the pelvis, up under the diaphragm, when a hospital security guard came uneasily into the room. She had put a gown over her uniform, shoe covers, OR hat, mask, all a bit askew. A normally confident woman, pushed out of her comfort zone. Beth looked up, recognized her. "What's up, Anna Marie? Here to collect the evidence?"

"You know it, Dr Abernathy. Guy's a pedophile. Registered sex offender, out on parole. Dunno who shot him, but I bet he had it coming."

The medical student silently held out his hand to Beth. On the bloody palm of his glove lay a ragged cylinder of felt. The wadding.

After they resected the damaged bowel and made a last check for hemostasis, Beth backed away from the table, leaving the chief resident and student to close up. Kim nodded at her.

"Thanks, everyone," she said, leaving without waiting for a reply.

Kim joined her out at the scrub sink, leaving the patient to his own, very able, chief resident. Beth and Kim stood side by side, looking into the OR through the windows over the sinks. Once they had had coffee together after another tough case, and he had told her about his childhood flight from Korea into the West. Months of his childhood spent hiding from soldiers. From his own countrymen. Ultimately, a new life and safety in the UK. His father and mother, both physicians, opened a Korean grocery store and sent their son to Oxford, where he majored in Anatomy. He had wanted to be a surgeon, but had considered himself lucky to get an anesthesia residency at Cook County.

"This man's wife awaits you in the Surgical Intensive Care waiting room," Kim finally said. Beth drew a sharp breath. "You will be able to assure her that he is doing very well indeed," he continued. At their feet, three suction canisters full of blood sat waiting for proper disposal. She realized she had tracked blood out into the hall, and bent over to take off her OR booties.

"WTF," she muttered.

"I beg your pardon?"

"Just an old Bellevue expression. Wonder how she'll take the news."

She suddenly remembered looking outside their bedroom window after hearing the coyotes. Had it been just the previous morning? Or the day before? She had lost track. The fresh snow had been pock-marked with tracks, and there was a patch of blood on the snow where the coyotes had torn some small animal to pieces. A weasel, perhaps. A rabbit. Or maybe a house cat.

* * *

A week later, one of those late autumn warm spells blew in from Missouri, to the south, and she biked to work. She was racing along the river, the flat trail paralleling a major thruway, when she saw a car pulled over in the lane closest to her, facing her. She slowed and warily edged a bit farther away from the road.

Once, as an undergraduate, she'd responded to a man in a car pulled over on the shoulder of another thoroughfare running along another river in a different city. He'd pretended to ask directions, but as she leaned into the open passenger side window the rhythmic motion of his left hand drew her eye to his crotch and his unzipped fly. Even as she mechanically responded to his bogus query, she froze her expression and backed off, walking fast in a direction opposite to traffic so that he could not follow her. The tears and anger came out later, when she rejoined her boyfriend...

But this man was simply staring away from her, across two lanes of traffic, where a coyote walked slowly down the median strip towards incoming traffic. She stopped and dismounted her bike. The coyote had no business out there in daylight – was it rabid? It looked tired. Cars avoided, and when a long gap came in traffic, it edged over to the shoulder. There a steep grassy slope led to a wooded area.

Beth tried to will the animal to run up the slope, out of danger. Its coat was ragged and the slender muzzle was brindled with grey. It stepped briefly onto the rotten snow that edged the shoulder and stepped back, shaking its forefoot just a house cat might when going out, reluctantly, into the snow.

CLINIC DAY

Dr. Beth Abernathy stood in the middle of the hallway, studying the posted list of clinic patients. A group of medical students came chattering like bluejays down the hall towards her, then slipped single file behind her as silent as monks on their way to matins. She didn't budge, and she didn't look at them.

She had been up late the night before, operating, and had slipped her broad, gold wedding band into the breast pocket of her white coat. Now she noticed it was not on her finger. She absently fished into the pocket with her left hand, pulled the ring out, and slipped it on. The wedding band and her broad, gold hoop earrings gleamed dully against her lightly tanned skin.

She frowned slightly as she read the clinic list. Twenty-seven patients in all, 13 before lunch, if she even had time for lunch, and then 14 after. And probably a couple of add-ons. She turned suddenly on the ball of her right foot with a swirl of her pleated skirt, and headed into the first exam room. Margaret, her clinic nurse, broke free from a group talking in the corner of the room and hastily followed her, clutching a clipboard. Clinic had begun.

An hour later, she and Margaret sat facing a young woman who wanted the lump out. Now. Never mind that it was benign by clinical, imaging, and even needle biopsy criteria. It was a lump, and she wanted it out. There was no point in arguing, Beth reminded herself. When she was a medical student, it was standard practice to remove every palpable lump. And the operations were all done under general anesthesia, with the woman's consent ahead of time for a mastectomy if necessary. Many women went to sleep under anesthesia wondering if they would have two breasts or one when they woke up. The bad old days.

And, who knows, the lump might not be benign after all. And even benign fibroadenomas sometimes grow, especially when a woman became pregnant. Best just to take it out. Margaret went ahead and started the paperwork to book the case in the Minor Surgery Suite, and Beth moved on to the next patient.

It was shortly after noon when Beth opened the door to exam room #10. Clinic was running behind schedule, as usual. Behind the curtain, a small woman sat on the exam table, her bare upper half covered by a once-mauve Breast Clinic poncho faded to dingy grey. Square diamond earrings and a very good makeup job, golden hair done in a smooth twist. Husband looked like a businessman, Brooks Brothers suit, sat in a chair in the corner. Mammograms were hanging on the x-ray view box and Beth could see the problem from clear across the room.

Putting the chart down on the tiny desk, Beth smiled and introduced herself, logged onto the computer, opened a new patient file. Sarah Langenberg. Margaret had already filled out the Breast Clinic data sheet, and in theory everything she needed to know was already there. But not really everything. Patients sometimes remembered new information the second time around.

And somehow it just never felt right to start right off with the exam. Asking the questions helped build rapport. Usually. As if verifying the information, she asked:

"Fifty-one years old?"

A pained frown. "Yes."

"And you found a lump in your breast?"

"He found it, actually," a shrug of the head toward the husband, who straightened just a bit and touched the knot of his tie.

"How long ago?" Two weeks, it said on the form. The questions went on through family history (none), past history, gynecologic history (they had two children, she had not breast-fed), and finally The Last Question. Margaret opened the door, slipped inside with her clipboard. The woman looked dismissively at Margaret, then returned her glance to Beth.

Beth went on with her history, unfazed. "Is there anything I haven't asked about that you think might be related?" Beth always asked this one. Silly question, most people probably thought. But once in a while you hit pay dirt. She recalled one young woman who was sent to her for evaluation of severe, unremitting breast pain and who, in response to The Last Question, said "Well, I was raped a couple of years ago and he beat me pretty badly, especially around the breasts."

But, as often happened, this patient just looked puzzled as if Beth were unusually dense and said, "I don't think so. I just had my annual a month ago and my doctor didn't feel anything. But then *he* felt something, and they got this mammogram, and..." And then my troubles began, thought Beth, recalling the hero of *Maus*, who'd used that phrase to introduce his recollections of the Holocaust.

Margaret pulled the curtain so as to block the view in case someone opened the exam room door. Sarah started to lay down, but Margaret stopped her. "She'll examine you sitting up first," she said kindly. Beth washed her hands at the sink and turned to look. Lifted the poncho, which was little more than a square of heavy cloth with a hole for the head, kind of like a medical serape. A cloud of expensive scented soap, or maybe dusting powder, drifted into the air of the small room.

Doesn't she look at herself in the mirror? Beth wondered. One nipple's pulled up and in. Bad business.

"Raise your arms up over your head" – doing this herself, so that Sarah would know what to do. The nipple pulled up even more, tethered by some sinister thing under the surface. Beth thought she could see a mass.

"Put your hands at your sides and push in – like this" – showing her, again. Simon says, she thought. Simon says arms up, Simon says push in...

"Now leave your hands where they are, but relax the muscles. Let them go limp." Confused, Sarah dropped her arms to her sides. Beth thought ruefully, about half of them do that. She wondered how you could say it differently, get them to do what you wanted them to do. She put Sarah's hands back on her hips, so that the axillary area was accessible, and dug her hands up into the armpits, feeling for axillary lymph nodes. Felt the firm lumps under the left arm. Matted. Fixed.

She had Sarah lay down and felt the breasts. The mass itself was surprisingly difficult to feel - Sarah had firm, lumpy breasts and had neglected to mention she had had breast implants, even though they were clearly visible on the mammogram. Well, Beth thought, maybe these implants went in before she met hubby? Don't poke that skunk, as the residents sometimes said. Give the man credit for finding the lump. No wonder the OB/GYN missed it. That's why you always *look* first. Sometimes the nipple retraction or skin retraction gives you the first clue. Chuck Steinberg had taught her that. Dead now, Chuck was, like so many of her old professors. She regretted not bringing the med student with her to see this patient.

She finished the exam quickly, running her fingers deliberately along the nearly invisible scars from the breast implants to let Sarah know that she was aware they were there. Our secret.

Margaret sat Sarah up as Beth circled back to the sink for another quick wash. Window-dressing, but it bought her time to think how to approach this one. Clinical stage IIB at least, she thought. Even if it's ER positive, she'll need chemotherapy. She'll lose that hair. No way we can save that breast. The implant's probably gotta go too. I should do a core needle biopsy, not a fine needle. That way I'll get enough tissue for receptors. Be careful not to pop the implant, even though it's coming out, eventually, just make her madder than she is already, if that's possible. The cafeteria closes in 10 minutes. I'm not going to make it to lunch.

Tightening her stomach muscles to suppress the growling of her stomach, Beth walked over to the view box and invited Sarah to come stand beside her. Sarah flicked the mauve drape sheet around her with unconscious elegance and came to stand just behind Beth – such a tiny thing, Beth noticed, that her head barely reached Beth's shoulder, even in heels. She held the drape sheet gathered in a fold at her neck with her left hand. Her fingers were long, her nails expertly French-manicured, the diamonds on the wedding band substantial, and the engagement ring beside it flashed. Beth felt old, clumsy, tired, sweaty, hungry.

"You can see the problem here. It's this shadow." Choosing the word with care, a gentler word, even than the term "mass" or "lump" or "tumor." The great white blotch sprawled crabwise across half of the left breast. Of course, with the implants, it was a bit tricky gauging the actual size, Beth thought. Must have a slide made of that mammo, for my teaching file. I wonder if she'd let me take a picture of her breast?

"You need a needle biopsy."

"You can do it next month when we come back from Scotland," the woman said.

"This can't wait," Beth replied.

The husband spoke then. A soft, gentle, cautious voice. "Honey, we don't need to go."

"But we always go. And there's that party we always give."

"We don't need to give it this year." Good man! He'd pulled a Levenger note pad out of his coat pocket and was starting to take notes with a Mont Blanc pen. An ally. She'd tell him, when the time was right, that he'd possibly saved his wife's life, finding that lump.

In the far corner, Margaret had pulled her own battered notebook out of her lab coat. Checking dates, Beth knew, as she ran through the usual routine. Allow two days for the final results of the fine needle aspiration cytology. Then a two-hour block of time in the main OR for a modified radical mastectomy, four hours if she wanted plastics to put in a tissue expander for another implant, six to eight hours if she wanted a TRAM flap.

But this time it might not go that way. This wasn't really surgical disease. I could cut as wide as I dare, and there would still probably be tumor cells at the margins. So the strategy would have to be different. Start with chemotherapy, then cut. Restage, re-evaluate, then operate.

Beth caught Margaret's eye, shook her head gently. Margaret nodded, slipped her notebook back into her pocket, edged out the door to call the medical oncologist who was in charge of the protocol. They would have to take this one step at a time. Some patients wanted to know everything all at once, some didn't want to know anything. They would have to lead this woman step by step.

Sarah slumped, becoming even smaller, and walked slowly back toward the exam table, then suddenly whirled on the ball of one high-heeled sandal – like a dancer! Glared at Beth, raised her hands – for an instant Beth thought about how sharp those lacquered nails looked – then Sarah suddenly gave up.

"It's just so damned inconvenient," she said.

Margaret spoke then, for the first time, and edged toward the patient. "Honey, we'll work around your schedule. Let's you and me figure out when we can do this little procedure. If we do the needle biopsy today, we can have the results in two days..." Beth slipped gratefully out.

WHO WILL CATCH ME
WHEN I FALL?

Beth's pager went off at 4:45 that afternoon. Call technically began at 5 pm, and she was in her office, not changed into scrubs yet, catching up on mail. It was Gilbert, the Burn Unit Director.

"Hi, Beth - want to give you a heads-up. I accepted a burn from Keokuk, probably get here around 7 pm. They're going to have to do some resuscitation before they ship her. She's 86 years old and her shawl caught fire when she was making herself a pot of tea. Clothes went up in flames. She's about a 40%-er but at her age, expected survival is zilch. I tried to get the doc in Keokuk to just keep her comfortable there, told him there wasn't anything we could for her here, but the family insists. I'd stick around, but my daughter has a cello recital tonight and I really need to be there. Can you admit her, get her tucked in? Fluids and morphine, you know the drill. I'll deal with the family in the morning. Sorry."

"No problem. Tell the burn nurses to call me when she arrives."

Soft rustlings from the corridor outside her office signaled day's end, as people packed up and headed home. The halls outside grew quiet. Streams of people crossed over to the parking garage across the street to head home. Beth turned on National Public Radio, and All Things Considered filled the silence. She sorted through emails, looked at her watch - 6:30 - time for dinner.

Down in the cafeteria, she joined her on-call team of residents and students, huddled together at one of the long tables near a window. Rufus, her chief resident for the night, planned to do a Trauma Fellowship when he finished his training.

"Anything brewing?" she asked the group.

"Deidre went to see a patient in the ER, a rule out appy. And there's been some kind of major accident on the interstate - four car pileup, or something..." Just then, five pagers went off in rapid succession. Trauma service pagers, gang-triggered by the doc in the ER. Five right hands automatically went to five belts.

A med student dialed the trauma voice mailbox, and obligingly held the receiver so Beth and the Rufus could listen as well. "Tri-County Ambulance is 5 minutes out with an approximately 30 year old unrestrained driver, multiple rollover, ejected about 20 feet. Unconscious at the scene. Pulse 140, BP 80 over palp, respirs 23. Satting at 98. GCS is 6-7. Bleeding actively from an obvious open right femur fracture, multiple facial lacerations, breath sounds are diminished on the left. Belly is rigid. He's intubated and they have two IV's wide open with Ringer's. There was a second car involved in the crash. Police report there are two more victims of the same accident. We don't know their condition at this time. We'll get back to you. This is a trauma activation, I repeat, trauma activation. ETA is five minutes. See you when you get here."

Beth sat down with her tray. The residents crammed as much dinner as possible into their mouths and stuffed their white coat pockets with leftovers. With the luxury of seniority, she'd allow them a ten minute head start. Time for them to sort things out, and time for her to finish her dinner in silence and relative comfort. She glanced at the clock, closed her eyes briefly, stretched her neck by tilting her head first one way and then the other, and then attacked her food.

Less than ten minutes later, she was down in Trauma Room #1. The trauma victim lay on the special "spine mobilizer" trauma bed. Someone had placed an airsplint on his fractured leg. Blood leaked out at the ankle and dripped to the floor. Open fracture - six hours to get that washed out and fixed, or the risk of infection skyrockets. The Orthopods were already there, edgy to get the patient to surgery. The paperwork read "Patient #35". They don't even know his name yet. She pulled on a pair of rubber gloves.

A bandage had been wrapped around his head. It was already blood soaked and small pools of blood had accumulated on the gurney at his head and feet. He was in a rigid cervical collar to prevent motion of the spine. The respiratory therapy technician was transferring the breathing tube down his trachea from a hand held bag-ventilation device to a more conventional mechanical respirator. Electrical leads were being switched from the portable LifePak to the wall monitor so that everyone could see his vital signs. Which were not great - his pulse was 120, BP 60. It should be the other way around. His eyes were swollen shut, the eyelids ballooned outward and bruised.

Beth elbowed her way to his abdomen and undid the straps which held him to the long spine board. Fragments of glass from the windshield mingled with his clothes. She brushed the glass away with a gloved hand. The senior ER nurse cut the clothes open along the front, peeling them back to completely expose him under the overhead warmer. His abdomen was rigid and distended. At least a couple of liters of blood in there.

"Hang two units of O-negative blood please. Pump it in." Beth said. She could hear the strain in her own voice, and willed herself to relax. Tension in the small resuscitation room was already high. Adrenalin made people move faster, made them more alert. Too much, and they made mistakes. She had to set the tone.

"Two units O-neg," someone echoed, and Beth heard the small blood bank refrigerator open. There would be hell to pay with the blood utilization committee if this guy's crit came back too high, but she wasn't going to take a chance. His BP was still hovering at 60.

"How much Ringer's has he gotten?" Beth asked.

"Four liters," Deidre, the mid-level resident, answered.

"Keep it running. What do we have for access?"

"We got two 14 gauge IV's, one in each antecubital, and we're setting up to put in a main drain."

"Where you gonna put it?"

"Right groin."

"What if he has a major venous injury?"

"Uh, we'll put another one in the left subclavian."

"Correct. We'll do both. You go for the subclavian, Deidre and I can do the groin."

Deirdre poured prep solution onto the groin, and Beth opened a sterile pack and pulled on sterile gloves. "Have you ever done one of these?" Beth asked.

"No."

"Seen one?"

"No."

"You help me do this one; you'll do the next. I don't know where the term 'main drain' originated, but that's what we called them at Bellevue. These lines were lifesavers in Viet Nam." As she talked, Beth opened the sterile cutdown pack. She took a knife and made a long oblique slash over the large vessels in the groin. The pulse in the femoral artery was fast and faint. The skin and fat barely bled - a bad sign! She spread the fat with the back of the scalpel handle, sweeping it up and down.

The saphenous vein popped into view easily - sometimes you get lucky. She passed a hemostat under it to elevate it. Deidre made a small nick in the vein with the knife and cannulated it with a large bore sterile polyethylene tubing, slipping it easily up into the femoral vein. Beth tied it in place. "You do the whole thing next time. Go ahead and close the wound and secure the line."

The two units of blood had run in so fast there wasn't time for the blood bank to send down the type-specific they'd requested. Hang more Ringers. Meanwhile Rufus had another good line in the right antecubital. Just in case the main drain was in a vein that led to a bleeding site.

"Be a shame if he had a caval disruption and those two units of blood had gone into his belly, wouldn't it?" she said to the med student. "All that good blood bank blood going out through a hole. Unlikely, but possible."

The technician slapped the chest x-ray on the view box. Even from across the room you could see the difference between both sides of the chest. The left side looked opaque, pale grey-white compared with the right. Hemothorax.

"Needs a chest tube! Now!" she barked automatically, but Rufus was already cracking the seals on the pack of instruments. The student drifted toward the x-ray view box.

"Do you see the findings?" Beth asked him.

"There's a pneumothorax on the right side?"

"Good guess, but not quite. Look here. See how it looks whiter on the left side than on the left, and how you can see the edge of the lung, where it's dropped away from the pleural lining of the chest wall. And look, the mediastinum is shifted a bit toward the right - that means there is pressure on the left. So why is that? Why does it look that way? What are we worried about with trauma patients?"

"Bleeding."

"Exactly. The film won't show you that nice straight line, like a waterline, that you see on an upright chest x-ray. We daren't sit him up because he could have a spine injury that might be made worse, remember we talked about that in our conference? So all you can see is that the left chest is whiter than the right, because the x-rays don't penetrate the blood as well as they do the lung. So we'll put a chest tube in to drain the blood and allow the lung to re-expand. He'll breathe better, and we can monitor the rate of bleeding better. If he is bleeding rapidly, we can even cleanse the blood and reinfuse it back into him through that big IV line - that's called autotransfusion. Often the bleeding will stop when the lung is reinflated. That's because blood flows through the lungs under very low pressure. If you can suck the lung up against the chest wall by evacuating the blood, the bleeding may stop."

Meanwhile, Rufus was guiding Deidre through the chest tube insertion. Beth edged closer to the gurney, just as Deidre poked into the chest with a hemostat. Blood gushed out.

"Spread, spread, make a big enough hole. Good. Good. Now stick your finger in and feel around. Feel the lung? The diaphragm? Yes? Good. Now the tube. Here it is." Rufus kept up a constant reassuring and instructional patter while watching every move.

Blood poured from the tube, dark blood, Beth noted. It sluiced over the sheet and onto the floor. Patient #35 needed that chest tube for sure.

"Hook it up, hook it up. Good. Good. Don't let it slip out. Now, here's a suture. You need to secure it in place."

"Good job," Beth said to no one in particular, eyeing the BP nervously. "Now, let's get him upstairs. Now! Call the OR and tell them we're coming. Now!"

She wondered what was going on with his head. Too early to tell. Brain won't work if the heart stops pumping...if he bleeds out. Stop the bleeding first, then figure it out. The best belly surgeon won't save him if he has a badly smashed brain. The brain was like jello, contained in a rigid box. Tethered at the bottom by the spinal cord and a stalk-like structure aptly termed the brainstem. Structures in the brainstem controlled vital functions like breathing and blood pressure as well as routing signals up and down to the spinal cord. The packaging was designed to withstand forces of the sort you might encounter if you tripped and fell. Accidents at highway speeds...force equals mass times acceleration...she shook her head. "We'll get a head CT when he stops bleeding" she said. "Any word on the other two victims?"

"Tri-County Ambulance says they're not as badly hurt."

She turned to the ER doc - "Sutherland's my backup. I'll alert her in case you need to call her in." Turning back to the team, "Let's go let's go let's go!"

She watched them go down the hall, Rufus leading the way, the med student pushing - vis a tergo – and took a separate path to the OR. One that led past the coffee machines. It was going to be a long night.

"Dr Abernathy – there's that possible appy," Deidre called after her.

"Start some fluids, check a urinalysis and a CBC, and get him admitted. The ER doc can help you. Come update us in the OR, we'll be there for a while. Tell the ER I'll come back down as soon as I can. Go on, go, go." She waved Deidre off without even turning to look back and plodded a slow and easy pace, a marathoner's pace, not a sprinter's, down the hall.

Five minutes later she stood outside OR room 10, the trauma room and stared through the windows into the room. Drained her coffee, watching the activity over the rim of the cup. She was pleased to see that they had gotten the crash victim's BP up to 110 and his heart rate down to 110. Vital signs almost uncrossed. Good move. They're about equal. Two more units of blood had been obtained and were running. Time to scrub up.

She took her position standing across the operating table from Rufus. Leaned into a comfortable stance, her pelvic bones leaning against the edge of the operating table, her legs set wide apart. Relaxed her shoulders. Adjusted the operating lights.

Rufus opened the abdomen with a long trauma incision from xiphoid to pubis, not stopping to cauterize the few bleeders. Patient #35 was still in profound shock. Entered the abdomen. Blood everywhere, half-clotted, half-fluid. It poured out, spilled out, lay between coils of bowel like badly-set cranberry Jello. It was too thick to suction, so they scooped it out, packed the abdomen off in quadrants.

The spleen was in fragments and bleeding badly. No time to save it - this spleen had to go. With a couple of clamps, they secured the major vessels at the splenic hilum. Rufus rapidly removed the shattered spleen. They irrigated and packed again. Liver had a laceration, but it was not bleeding significantly. They packed that as well. Irrigated some more. Not much else wrong - there was a pelvic hematoma from a fracture - leave that one alone. Needs an ex-fix, Ortho can take care of that when they fix his open fracture.

"I think we got the bleeding slowed down to a trickle. Have you guys caught up yet?" Rufus asked Anesthesia.

"More or less. He's starting to make a little urine."

"Time for the secondary survey." Beth told Jeremy. "Now we check and double check anything for missed injuries."

They methodically checked every quadrant, removed blood and clots from every nook and cranny, every peritoneal fold, washed and washed with liters of saline. The goal was discovery as much as cleanliness. They were looking for any evidence of continued bleeding. They irrigated until the effluent turned from cranberry juice to pink Kool Aid and finally returned clear in the suction tubing, and then packed with clean white laparotomy pads.

They inspected the entire bowel, inch by inch, looking for lacerations and mesenteric injuries. They checked the stomach, the duodenum, the pancreas. The colon and the appendix were fine, everything was fine. They rechecked the splenic bed for hemostasis, inspected the ligatures on the splenic artery and vein. The liver laceration had stopped bleeding. The clean white laparatomy pads came out with a few pinkish spots - blood diluted by irrigation fluid. Nothing was oozing.

Beth relaxed a little, stretched, and said, "Good. Looks good. No coagulopathy - we're lucky. Check your hemostasis one more time and close him up. Call Ortho, they can wash out that fracture when we're done. I'm going back to the ER, find out what's happening, Deidre should have been up here by now. Call if you need me. Get him settled in Recovery and talk to the family - is there any family?"

"Wife was also hurt. Took her to St Joseph's. Don't know much more."

Beth peeled off her glove and gown, reaching back and tearing the paper strips that held the back closed. 8:25. Time flies when you're having fun. Noted with dismay that the trousers of her scrub suit were soaked with blood from mid-shin to ankles. She hadn't even felt it happen. She was soaked with blood through to her skin. A stranger's blood, possibly tainted. She headed for the showers, clean scrubs, before going back down to the ER.

This time there were two patients in adjacent bays in the Trauma area. The couple who had been driving the other car. Both were wearing seat belts, and the airbags had deployed on impact. Deirdre and the ER doc had done the initial survey, found no major injuries. The wife was pregnant, about seven months. OB was already there checking her out. Mother and unborn child seemed to be fine.

"Do we have any family for Patient #35?" she asked the room in general.

"Mother and some brothers outside. And the name is Nichols. Want me to put them in the consult room? How's he doing?"

"We got the bleeding stopped. He's stable. I still don't know about his head. Please go ahead. Tell her I'll go talk with her in a moment." Beth turned to Deidre, "What's the story on the appy?"

Deidre filled her in. It was the real thing.

Beth nodded. "Go ahead and preop him. Call the OR. I'll go see him in a few minutes. Have to talk to the family of that trauma." She leaned heavily on the counter and scanned the ER. It was laid out in the old-fashioned way, so that a person standing at the control island could see what was going on in each of the cubicles without moving. She could see the kid with appendicitis curled up on a gurney, Mom and Dad at the bedside. The rest of the cubicles were empty, waiting for the late night rush. She gathered herself up and headed out of the ER to the hallway with the waiting room (empty) and the two consultation rooms. In the second consultation room, she saw a haggard-looking white haired woman and two hulking middle-aged men. "Are you with Mr Nichols?" she asked. One of the men started toward her, nodded yes.

She went in, sat down, and gestured for them to sit around her. Took a deep breath. "He is stable. We just finished operating on his belly. His spleen was ruptured, we had to remove it. We were able to repair some tears in his liver and stop all the bleeding. But he has several fractures and a severe head injury. We had to take him straight up to surgery before we could do the scans to determine how bad the injury to his head is. The orthopedic surgeons are treating his leg. The neurosurgeons will assess him in the ICU. He is in very critical condition."

"But he's going to live, isn't he?" the mother asked.

Another deep breath. "I hope so. But at this point I really don't know the full extent of his injuries. He was thrown from his car and went about twenty feet through the air before he landed. If he landed on his head, well, you can imagine how bad the injury can be. We just don't know at this point. He came through surgery OK and that's the first step. The bleeding is under control. Now we can assess the other injuries. We'll just have to see."

A brother interjected, "his wife is at St Joseph's. She's got a broken leg. They're going to keep her overnight. What should I tell her?"

"Tell her what I just said. He's very critical right now. We'll know a lot more in the next 24 hours." She added, "you're welcome to stay in this room if you wish, until he goes up to the SICU. Then you'll be able to see him. He's going to look terribly bruised and swollen, and there will be all kinds of tubes in him. He'll be on a breathing machine, and he may be in traction. Just remember, we're doing everything we can for him."

Back in the ER, she confirmed that the kid did, indeed have appendicitis. The OR was backed up with other cases and it would be a while before they could do his surgery.

Beth's pager went off again. The Burn Unit. She dialed the number by memory.

"Beth, your burned lady is here. We're in resuscitation room 2. She's stable, intubated, making urine. Rufus is up here with us. He's got things under control. Family hasn't arrived yet."

"I'll be up in five minutes."

She looked over the labs on the appy, and added a brief note at the bottom of Deidre's documentation. She turned to Deirdre and said, "I've got to go up to the Burn Unit. You stay with this kid and page me when he's on the table."

"OK."

Up in the Burn Unit, Rufus and the burn nurses already had the old lady swaddled in silvadene ointment and gauze dressings. She was breathing comfortably on the ventilator, and did not seem to be in any pain. There was a trickle of urine in the catheter bag. Beth picked up the old lady's hand. Skin thin as oiled silk barely hid the bones and tendons underneath.

Beth said, "Gilbert's my back up tonight. He'll come in if you need him. If you get any more traumas, call him." Rufus nodded.

He said slowly, "You know, this lady's just about the age of my grandma. Looks kind of like her, too."

She nodded and said, "yeah, well, it costs money to make clothes flame-proof. The law says that clothes for children must be flame-proof, but there isn't any requirement for clothes for adults. So little old ladies set themselves on fire when they reach over to get the teapot off the gas stove. Make sure your grandma has an electric stove, and tell her not to wear her shawl, or anything with trailing sleeves, when she goes near it."

Beth took the back stairs down to the call room. Lay down and put her feet up. Must have fallen asleep, because the next thing she knew the pager was going off again. The OR.

* * *

An hour later, the appendix was out, and the child was on his way to the Recovery Room. Beth drained the last of her hot chocolate in two long gulps and went looking for the boy's mother.

* * *

She was just drifting off to sleep in the call room when her pager went off again.

"Sorry, Dr Abernathy, but Mrs Austen's family just got here. Do you have a few minutes to talk to them?"

"Sure. Put them in the waiting room. I'll be up in five."

Beth gently set the handset back onto the cradle of the phone, and leaned against the desk, head bowed. She had hoped to avoid this. She hated this part of the job. She started walking toward the Burn Unit, wondering how she was going to tell this family that grandma wasn't going to make it? They brought her here, to Buckthorne, because we work miracles, Beth thought. But there was no miracle for an old lady that severely burned. No kindness in keeping her alive, putting her through days of pain, with nothing at the end. Even if she survived, by some miracle, she'd end up in a nursing home.

She could always let Gilbert break the news. He said he would take care of it, after all. But it was her tour of duty, and they were here now. It was only 3 am.

She walked up the stairs to the waiting room outside the Burn Unit. Inside, an elderly farmer in a John Deere cap and bib overalls waited next to two middle aged couples. Mrs Austen's husband and their grown children probably. Beth took a deep breath, walked in, and introduced herself. She pulled up a footstool and sat directly in front of Mr Austen.

Took his big wide hands in hers. The ring and little fingers were missing from the right hand. Were she to ask, he'd probably say it was an old farm accident. Bandsaw, maybe. Took off the guard. Fed it through by hand, instead of using another piece of wood. Got a little too close one time. Half-buried in the thick skin of the left hand, a narrow wedding band, worn thin with years, gleamed dully.

"Mr Austen, we have a problem. Your wife was very badly burned."

"I know that. I was the one who put her out. Wrapped a blanket around her, called the ambulance."

"You did exactly right, but – her burns are very deep. She'll need lots of painful wound care and several operations. And she probably won't make it. It's almost impossible for someone her age to survive a burn this bad. Heart and lungs just won't take it. We're keeping her comfortable now, she's not in any pain. That's the kindest thing we can do. Did your wife have an advance directive? What some people call a living will?"

"Yup. We both signed them. She doesn't want to be on life support."

"She's not on life support. We're giving her fluids into her vein, that's all. We'll get her settled and let you be with her. We'll keep her comfortable."

He nodded slowly. "Been married 64 years." He turned to the older son.

"Dad, a guy at my plant got burned. Not even this bad. He was in the hospital a month and he told me later he never felt such pain. Got scars you can see to this day." The son turned toward Beth and added, "Dr Abernathy, we all love her. But none of us want her to suffer. Please keep her comfortable."

"We will. We will."

The farmer looked back at Beth. "Been married 64 years. High school sweetheart. What am I going to do?" The middle-aged woman next to him, a daughter maybe, enfolded him.

He remained defiantly upright, refused to return the embrace, glared at Beth.

"We'll keep her comfortable, I promise. I'll tell the nurses to let you see her just as soon as they can."

Beth leaned back slightly, gently releasing Mr Austin's hand. Sometimes she thought she was growing a shell, like an old Galapagos tortoise. Thicker and thicker every year. Defense against all the pain she saw every day. Or maybe it was a crystalline cocoon, like a coffin. She could see out, but she couldn't break out. When the process was finished, what would remain? What would she be able to see, to feel? She stood up and drew back into that cocoon now, turned her back on the old farmer and walked away.

Beth stopped at the food machines on her way back to the call room. It was almost 6 am. Milk and cookies looked good. She had barely enough change. Counted it out carefully, yes, just enough. She lay on the bed and pulled out her journal. Wrote for a few minutes.

Call night almost over. One appendix removed. One brain-injured trauma. An old woman who's going to die. Husband pole-axed. Why tonight? Why tonight?

She set the pen down. Saw a silvery mist, tenuous. Trees. The mist became a film, a membrane, coming toward her, pushing, pushing. A fist appeared, infinitesimally slowly pushing toward her through the membrane, which stretched over the knuckles. She was frozen. Unable to move. Wanted to scream. Nothing came out.

A knock on the door. "Housekeeping". She must have fallen asleep. Time to get up. In most specialties the on-call physician went home the next morning, but that had never been the tradition in surgery. Besides, female surgeons always had to be stronger, more macho than anyone else. So, feeling faintly nauseated, she stalked grimly into the call-room bathroom, and pulled off her scrubs, walked into the shower. Let it run. Shampooed her hair, toweled it dry, put on clean scrubs and packed up her gear.

In the office, she brewed some real coffee, and added a bit of mocha flavoring for a treat. Put her feet up on the desk and listened to NPR's Morning Edition. Nothing major seemed to have happened overnight. More skirmishes in the Middle East. It might snow tomorrow. She looked at her calendar. Clinic until 5 pm, then make rounds, get home early (maybe). Don't even think about the possibility.

* * *

The group gathered for afternoon rounds outside the SICU. Beth was the first to speak. "So tell me about Nichols. How's he doing?"

"He's hemodynamically stable, but he hasn't shown any signs of neurologic recovery. The SICU staff and neurosurgery think he's neurologically devastated. Did you see his CT scan?"

"No. Diffuse axonal injury, I was told."

"That's right. A bad one. Nothing to relieve by surgery. Brain is mush. Must have hit the ground hard."

"Fly twenty feet through the air and see how light you land. Especially when you were ejected from a car going 65 mph to start with. Too damn bad. We fixed everything else."

They had paused on the landing opposite the Burn Unit. Beth thought about Mrs Austen, the old lady with the bad burns. She started toward the door leading to the Burn Unit and said, "Get the CT scan and tell Rufus I'll meet you both in the SICU in five minutes. I just want to check on a patient from last night."

A housekeeping aide passed Beth as she went over to Mrs Austen's cubicle. Wintry light flooded the immaculate empty room. The bed was stripped and made up with clean white linens, ready for the next patient. Beth went up to the bed and leaned on the bedrails, lowering her head and closing her eyes for a moment.

She was not particularly religious, but at moments like this she would sometimes try to send a prayer out, for the living, that somehow they would find peace. When she looked up, Beth saw something the housekeeper had missed. A small note, written in crayon, and taped to an IV pole where someone lying in bed could read it. "I love you Grandma" it said. She peeled the note off, looked at it for a moment, and put it carefully in her pocket. She stood resting against the doorjam for a moment, then turned and took the back stairs down to SICU.

* * *

In the SICU, the Critical Care team had just finished putting a new central line in Nichols. They gathered up their equipment and waved her in. She pulled back the sheet and gently felt Nichols' belly. No response. The belly was swollen, but soft. A neat narrow white bandage covered his incision. No blood had seeped through. Her part of his care was still holding. He was in a rigid cervical collar to protect his spine. They hadn't done all the x-rays needed to prove that his neck wasn't broken. Really didn't matter at this point. Both eyelids were swollen shut, eyelids protruding like over-ripe plums from the orbits. Tubes were taped in place with clean tape. Someone had washed the blood out of his hair and cut it short in places where it couldn't be combed clean. He lay on a clean white pillow.

They reviewed his head CT scan in silence. Nothing to fix. Badly bruised brain. Take something the consistency of partially congealed gelatin, enclosed in a rigid container, and throw it

20 feet and that's what you end up with. DAI - diffuse axonal injury - fibers stretched and broken, connections severed, nerve cells killed. Broken brain. Can't be fixed. The soul off wandering somewhere, and we can't call it back. She thought about the ending of <u>Buddenbrooks</u>, where the small boy dies because his soul, wandering in fever, didn't want to come back. But this soul couldn't find its way back even if it wanted to. Best to let him go. A slender tube snaking from the top of his head led to a pressure monitor. The pressure reading was way too high, and they had tried every trick in the book to bring it down. That pressure would kill any remaining uninjured brain cells, force the brain stem out through the tentorial notch like toothpaste out of a tube...

"Has anyone talked with his wife?"

"She's still in St Joseph's. The mom says she's due for release later today."

* * *

An hour later, she was paged back to SICU.

"Mrs Nichols is here. You wanted to talk to her."

"Yes. I'm on my way."

Multiple tubes and devices still surrounded Nichols, but the nurses had created a niche to one side where Mrs Nichols could bring her wheelchair close enough to hold one of his hands. They had matching wedding bands, Beth noticed. Mrs Nichols right leg was in a short leg cast, and she had a nicely sutured facial laceration and a black eye, but she looked pretty good. Beth went into the cubicle and introduced herself.

"Mrs Nichols? I'm Dr Abernathy." The woman turned, and smiled the easy warm smile of a woman who lived to make others happy. Beth had a sudden image of a nicely kept home, warm food on the table, children tucked in at night, shirts ironed, a garden full of flowers and nice ripe tomatoes. The smile went straight to Beth's heart, and the crystalline shell snapped tight around her.

"Yes?" The woman's smile faded.

"I'm the surgeon on duty from last night. I operated on your husband, and I've been following as the Intensive Care team takes care of him now. May I sit down?"

"Please. How's he doing? The nurse says his blood pressure is good."

"Yes. His heart and lungs are fine, he has a good strong heart, but he took a terrible blow to his head. Our scan showed significant brain damage. And he hasn't shown any sign of recovery." She leaned forward. "We may have to make some difficult decisions." We. Not you. Although in truth it would be Mrs Nichols who would have the final say. Beth went on. "Is anyone here with you? Any family?"

Mrs Nichols shook her head. "Our youngest daughter's in college back East. Wellesley. I told her to stay there. Our son's in Chicago but he's got a job."

"You might want to have him join you."

Mrs Nichols nodded slowly, lips compressing to a thin horizontal line.

"Here's my card. They can get in touch with me anytime you need me. We'll talk again tomorrow. Do you have any questions?"

* * *

Jonathan hung up the phone. Another late night. This made three, so far, this week. And Beth had sounded on edge. He wondered if she'd tell him what happened. He'd learned not to ask her. She rarely talked about work anymore. At night, she slept like a stone, never hearing their cat, Ninja, the wind, or sleet on the skylight.

When she was a surgical resident, she would sleep so heavily that she'd awaken with an arm or leg temporarily gone flail because she didn't shift in her sleep as most people did. Once she awoke unable to see clearly out of one eye, only to realize that the pressure of her arm, flung across her eyes, had temporarily flattened her cornea. Then, too, those days she would fall asleep waiting for supper to be set in front of her. He had thought then that she must love surgery very much, to put up with the hours she did during her residency. He wondered now if she still did.

* * *

Jonathan was already asleep when she got home. He'd left the outdoor lights on, and there was a frozen dinner loaded into the microwave, ready to go. He'd pre-programmed the microwave oven. All she had to do was hit the start button, wait a few minutes, and eat.

After dinner, too tired to go upstairs to bed right away, and still a bit wired from the past 36 hours, Beth sat nursing her cup of decaf. Pumpernickel and Ninja licked the last scraps from the frozen dinner tray, chasing the light plastic container around the kitchen. Finally lost it behind a trash can. Ninja looked around, walked out of the kitchen, cat on a mission, looking for mice. The Weather Channel flickered on the TV screen, sound turned off. Rain beat against the kitchen windows, sending rivulets glinting against the black of the night, and sometimes carrying the flinty sound of embedded sleet.

Ninja stalked restlessly into the kitchen, having assured himself that the rest of the house was free from mice. Came and stood by her feet, yowled. Beth sat immobile, her gaze passing through the TV screen, eyes focused somewhere beyond.

She didn't see the clean vaulting leap that brought Ninja to the countertop next to the refrigerator, but it was impossible to miss the attempt at free flight that followed as he aimed for the top of the fridge. The laws of physics were against him. It wasn't that he failed in the ascent, but rather that he couldn't put on the brakes in time. He slid from his landing point across the smooth top of the fridge, claws scrabbling in frantic but futile attempt at purchase. Ninja and the glass salad bowl both landed on the floor.

Beth looked up, heart pounding, her train of thought completely shattered. Ninja sprawled completely motionless on the kitchen floor. He wasn't breathing. The salad bowl had broken cleanly into two unequal parts. She ran down the trauma surgeon's laundry list of potential injuries. Subdural hematoma. Epidural hematoma. Ruptured spleen. Paraplegia. Quadraplegia. Cats can learn to walk again after a complete spinal cord injury, the lower motor centers taking over. But it's a lengthy process. Is he even alive? She couldn't tell.

She pressed her right hand lightly against his chest, wrapping the flats of her fingers around his slender elastic ribcage. Felt a fluttering, Ninja's heart beating, fast but strong. She was afraid to move him. No visible injuries. So small. A long minute passed. Ninja took a big breath, looked around, flicked his tail, started to lick himself. She gathered him up into her arms and pressed him to her chest.

"You stupid cat. You stupid cat." She sat crying alone in the empty kitchen, hugging the cat.

MISCONCEPTIONS

P lanned Parenthood would not give Brandi Dunbar oral contraceptives until we cleared her in Breast clinic. We get two or three of these referrals a month. The vast majority have benign lumps, the kind of thing we called fibrocystic disease. Brandi's mammogram report suggested this was something worse. I knocked, and entered the exam room.

Brandi sat hunched over on the foot of the exam table. A faded Breast Clinic poncho hung over her shoulders. The chart said she was 34. I would have guessed she was in her mid-forties. I introduced myself and held out my hand; she didn't reach out to shake it, so after a moment I withdrew my hand and sat down at the desk. I opened a new record on the computer and started taking her history.

"How long have you had this lump?"

"I don't know."

"Does it hurt?"

Shrug. "Only when you mash on it. So, do I get my pills?"

I asked about her family. There wasn't much else to the story. Brandi hadn't been in contact with her mother in almost 20 years and didn't know if her mom had had cancer or not. Her father had been out of the picture since Brandi was three. I put "unknown" in the blank after family history. Brandi herself had dropped out of school in 10th grade when she became pregnant. Her baby was put up for adoption, and Brandi had worked at a series of jobs. She had never married, and was currently unemployed. When I asked her the last time she'd seen a doctor, she said, "The last time I got shot."

As I washed my hands before examining Brandi, I looked over toward her, hoping to meet her gaze. She stared at her toes. The lobe of her left ear was notched, where an earring had pulled through some time ago. Maybe she wanted to leave it as it was. Or maybe she couldn't find a plastic surgeon who would operate for Medicaid rates. I made a mental note to ask my friend over in Plastics if she would take Brandi on. After we took care of the cancer.

When I lifted the poncho, I could see that the right nipple was flattened compared with the left. From just under the right nipple, a nasty-feeling lump spidered outward to occupy almost one quarter of her breast. The other breast was normal. I felt under her arms for axillary lymph nodes, first port of call when breast cancer starts to spread, and felt what could have been a node or two. But she had the scars of a botched tattoo removal on that shoulder, so maybe those nodes were innocent

Her mammogram showed two white splotches, a large one linked by delicate tendrils to a smaller adjacent one. I drew a circle on her breast with a skin marker and sent her down the hallway to Cytopathology, where they stuck a fine needle into the mass and drew out cancer cells. I went down the hall myself to look at the cells under the microscope with the pathologist. Magnified several hundred times, the cells were ugly cornflower-blue things – large, disordered, each different from the other, dividing wildly. Her right breast would have to go.

An hour later, those mammograms hung over the small desk in the exam room. I showed Brandi her films, talked about the diagnosis, and the surgery she needed. Why she needed a mastectomy instead of a lumpectomy. Brandi was unmarried, unemployed, and no one had come to clinic with her.

"I need a cigarette."

"In a minute. Just let me finish. You'll be in the hospital overnight after surgery. A week later, when we get the pathology report back, we can talk about further treatment. You're young – we want to give you the very best chance of a cure that we can. You'll probably need chemotherapy after your incision heals…"

But it was clear that Brandi wasn't listening, so I sent her outside for a smoke and then brought her back to a consult room to talk things over.

I went to see another new patient and almost forgot about Brandi until my clinic nurse reminded me. Brandi had changed into a Harley Davidson sweatshirt and was sitting up a bit straighter in that than she had in our Breast Clinic poncho. The claustrophobic consult room was heavy with cigarette smoke from her breath.

I showed her the mammogram again. Repeated my explanations until I knew that she had finally heard me. She ignored the box of tissues I passed to her, and angrily wiped her eyes and nose on the sleeve of her sweatshirt.

I waited for a few seconds, and then passed her the pen and consent for surgery.

* * *

When I unlocked the front door that evening, our old cat Pumpernickel trotted over to greet me. Her ears were already notched from old fights when we adopted her, half-grown and pregnant, and she has a scar next to her left eye from a near-miss. They say the winner has scars on her face, and the loser has scars on her butt — with cats, anyhow. I'd seen over 30 patients that day, but it was Brandi who came to mind as I sat at the kitchen table, stroking Pumpernickel and talking with my husband.

* * *

Brandi's surgery took longer than we expected. When I removed one of the nodes to test it, I knew I'd been right. It was plump, hard, irregular. The pathologist confirmed what I'd suspected - it was choked with tumor. We carefully dissected out the rest of the axillary nodes, shelled out her cancerous breast, and put in drains.

After the last stitch had been placed, I stepped back from the OR table with a sigh.

No one was waiting for her in our post-surgery waiting area.

After surgery Brandi cursed the nurses and refused morphine. When we rounded on her early the following morning, Brandi was AWOL and a strange man was asleep in her bed. Up until this point, Brandi had been alone. No one in the waiting room after her surgery. No family, no friends, no stuffed animals, no flowers at the bedside. Not even a card. When we woke the man up, he rubbed his eyes and said, "She went out for a smoke," and pulled the ragged hospital blanket up over his head to shut out the light.

An hour later the nurses paged me. Brandi had returned from her smoke, pushing her IV pole, a man's heavy leather jacket over her hospital robe. I walked over to the ward. As I paused to wash my hands at the sink in her room, I could hear voices through the curtains around her bed.

"Why didn't you tell me, babe? I'd have been there."

"Didn't want you to know. How'd you find out?"

"Poochie called me. Said you asked him to feed the dog, but he couldn't find the dog food. I rode nearly all night to get here. Damn, babe, why'd you call Poochie instead of me?"

Silence.

I knocked on the wall and opened the curtains. They were sitting side by side on the edge of the bed. His arm was around her, and she didn't look up when I walked in.

I changed her dressing and sent her home with instructions for wound care. The guy pulled a battered spiral notepad out of his pocket and wrote these down carefully with the stub of a pencil while Brandi stared past me out the window. The first snow of the season was falling.

* * *

Three weeks later, in clinic, I had to take Brandi by the shoulders and physically walk her over to the small mirror over the sink. By then, I had gotten to know the guy because he came with her to her clinic visits. His name was Jerome. He wore a bandanna tied over his head, looked me straight in the eye and did most of the talking. He asked questions and wrote down everything I said. I thought about telling him that sometimes people bring little tape recorders and tape the whole thing, and that was okay with me, if he wanted to do it. Jerome probably would have written that down too, and then gone out and bought one. But I worried that they might need the money for rent, or food. So I simply repeated myself slowly and clearly until he had it all down.

I was glad Brandi wasn't alone. When I lifted her poncho to examine her wound, she averted her eyes. Waiting behind a curtain, Jerome said, "Doc, I keep telling her I don't care. But she just won't look at herself."

"Look," I said to her. "Your wound is healing well. It will be completely hidden by your clothes. Once we get you through this, you can think about reconstructive surgery." Then, standing behind this small, slumping woman, I had also looked into the mirror. Brandi's eyes were downcast, fixed upon the slow drip of water falling from the single tap. I glanced down as well, and found myself staring at the dark stripe along the part in her coarse straw-colored hair. I stepped back, and let Brandi turn away and cover up her bare chest with the frayed off-white Breast Clinic poncho.

"There's something coming out here, where this red spot is," Brandi said suddenly, lifting the poncho to show me.

Gotcha! I thought, *you have sneaked a peek!* But I smothered my smile, and carefully cleaned the area, snipping the errant end of a buried suture. Her little victory, not letting me or Jerome know she had looked.

The lymph nodes were indeed positive, and so Brandi needed an access port placed for intravenous chemotherapy. I explained all this to her as gently as I could. Jerome wrote it all down in his little notebook, and said, "I don't care if you lose your hair, babe, you can get a wig. Any color you want. Go bald. I'll shave my own head. Doesn't matter to me."

Silent as always, eyes downcast, she signed the consent form for this minor surgical procedure without reading it first. I looked down at her childish signature, written slowly in a large round hand with a little heart drawn where the "i" in Brandi should have been dotted.

* * *

On the morning of this second operation, I was trying to graciously disentangle myself from a clot of secretaries with a baby when my pager went off. The baby hesitated for an instant, one slobbery small fist just inches from my glasses, and I fled into my office. I closed the door, took a deep breath, and pulled out my pager. A text page. "Dunbar for first case reports menses 20 days late. We are checking urine HCG." Surely Brandi wasn't pregnant.

* * *

I was halfway through my coffee and scan of the CNN website when I received another text message with an update. "Pregnant. Anesthesia wants to know what we want to do. Please call x4515."

Why do kids put beans in their ears, I thought – because no one told them not to. Had I warned her not to get pregnant? Even considered the possibility? I suddenly remembered her question, that first day in clinic, "So, can I have the pills?" Remembered Jerome, in her bed, that first morning after surgery.

My thoughts raced ahead, anticipating the next issues. Chemotherapy this early in pregnancy - it would be tough. We couldn't afford to wait until after Brandi delivered. By that time, the cancer would have had more than eight months to spread. Termination of pregnancy would simplify the situation considerably, particularly with a difficult patient. But it wasn't a step to be taken lightly.

I stood up and called the extension, told them I was on my way. The small group of women and the baby had moved on by the time I emerged from my office to head over to the pre-surgery unit. I had a plan. Cancel surgery, let Brandi think things over and come to an informed decision. Informed decision – had Brandi had really understood any of the things that had happened to her after she felt that lump in her breast? Fortunately, her medical oncologist was one of my favorites – an older man with infinite patience.

I approached Brandi's bed and elbowed through the small huddle – Jerome, the surgical resident, the anesthesiologist, and a nurse – to get close enough to speak with her. Before I could say anything, Brandi said, "I'm not going to let you do anything to hurt my baby. I don't believe in abortion."

I felt a flash of anger. I thought of asking Brandi if she planned to stop smoking, now that she was pregnant. Start wearing a helmet when she rode that big Harley behind Jerome, arms around his waist. But I just held up both hands and said, "Nobody's talking about abortion." Then I wondered what they had told her before I got there.

Jerome said, "Now babe, all I care about is you."

Brandi turned on him then, and said, "You're always talking about how you want a kid. Well, now, here you've got one." Her arms were curled protectively around her lower abdomen, still flat under the blankets. She looked back at me. I could see hazel flecks in her irises. She held my gaze directly, with a defiant resolve that I had never seen in her before.

Jerome said, "Someday. I want a kid someday."

I stood up straight, shifted my gaze from Brandi to Jerome, and said, "We'll all work through this together." I looked back at Brandi's clear eyes and said, "You know, it's going to be very important that you work with us. We need to get you treated. We can treat you and do our best to protect your baby, but you need to work with us. We want you to live to see your kid graduate from high school."

Jerome said, "Yeah, babe, we can get through this." Brandi just watched me with the wariness of a pregnant alley cat. I thought about Jerome and his notebook, his questions, how he always wrote down everything, how he was careful to get it all straight. I went over to the nurses' station and called her medical oncologist. We sent them over to his office from the preoperative holding area, after we got them some breakfast.

A TEACHING HOSPITAL

D r Beth Abernathy backed into the operating room, scrubbed hands held high, then turned to survey the situation. A frail old man lay on the operating table, distended abdomen painted brown with iodine prep solution. The junior resident stood at the wall telephone, saying, "...a colostomy. With The Old Lady. Yeah. About an hour." He looked up and saw her.

She stared past him at the X-ray view box. She had seen the films just an hour earlier, down in the emergency center. Hugely dilated colon, ballooning cecum, with no gas beyond the pelvic brim. Probably a sigmoid carcinoma. Maybe a diverticular stricture. Whatever. He needed an emergency colostomy to provide a vent for the accumulating stool and bowel gas.

Just minutes later, the resident joined her at the operating table and they began the operation. Layer by layer, they cut through enveloping fat, fascia and muscles until tensely swollen colon bulged out into the small incision, a fetid balloon about to burst.

"Four-O silk suture," Beth said to the scrub nurse. To the resident she added, "You'll need to decompress the colon first to minimize the chance of spilling stool. Place a four-bite, purse-string suture here."

He slowly and carefully guided the small curved needle through the bowel, taking four bites which outlined a small box. Beth suddenly remembered the Hospital Director complaining about her operative times. "It's a teaching hospital," Beth had said. "So teach faster," he shot back. *Screw you*, she thought.

Beth lifted the colon carefully with two atraumatic forceps, ready for the resident to incise the center of the purse-string with a scalpel. She looked over at the scrub tech and said, "Now, be ready with the suction catheter. There may be some stool."

Just then there was a flash of blue flame and a sound like "whup". Beth automatically put her hand down on top of the small incision, the teaching surgeon's response to any misadventure in the surgical field. Her gloved hand smothered the flame instantly. There was little heat, and remarkably little smoke. The resident looked dazed. He still had the electrocautery wand in his hand.

"Oh shit! I thought I taught you – never, never, never cut into the bowel with electrocautery," Beth said.

"Dr. Gilbert does it all the time. He says it prevents bleeding." Gilbert had just joined the faculty, fresh from the best trauma fellowship in the country.

"I don't give a rat's ass who does it. You can see why it's a bad idea. People have died from this!" She took the suction catheter away from the tech and cautiously moved her hand away from the loop of colon. Stool poured from the bowel, and the room filled with the aroma of bowel gas.

The resident stood like a statue, afraid to move. The small explosion had blown a ragged, silver-dollar sized hole in the side of the colon. The purse-string suture was gone, probably vapor-ized. The edges of the drapes were singed, and the sides of the gash in the colon looked dusky but viable.

Beth stuffed the metal suction tube into the gaping hole in the colon and the colon deflated. Despite the suction, stool con-tinued to pour over the edges of the bowel – the accumulation of days of increasing obstruction, now relieved.

"Bowel gas ignited," she said to no one in particular. "Meth-ane, probably. Happens sometimes. That's why you should never use electrocautery to open the bowel," she said, glaring at the resident. "We need to debride the bowel edges and assess the damage. Hopefully the rest of the bowel is OK."

Half an hour later, Beth backed away from the table, taking off gloves and gown as she headed for the scrub sink. Suddenly she felt both terribly thirsty and slightly nauseated. She pushed back her surgical cap from her forehead, removed her glasses, and splashed water on her face. She cupped her hands under the stream of water from the scrub sink faucet and drank her fill. Mercifully, her nausea abated.

She wiped her face with a paper towel and paused to look in the small mirror next to scrub sink. A few wisps of gray hair had emerged from the control of her cap and sagged wetly down her forehead. Her skin was ashen in the fluorescent lights, and she noticed, once again, how easy it had become to see the deli-cate veins through the skin of her eyelids. Something brown was stuck to her left eyebrow. She picked at it. Stool. From the explo-sion. She scrubbed her face again with iodine scrub solution and went into the women's locker room for a hot shower.

She felt completely alive, the water sluicing over her, washing sweat and stool alike down the drain. Her nausea was gone, and she felt a savage sense of vindication. *I told him not to do that,* she thought. *Now maybe they'll stop laughing at some of my habits.* Had she ever warned this particular resident? But there had been so many residents over the years. A career spanning almost four decades.

She slithered into clean scrubs, adjusted her cap, and went to the recovery room to check on the patient.

It was always a bit of a shock when she saw the patient who had been underneath the drapes. Under the OR lights, it was easy to forget about the person under the blade. Her patient was just starting to breath for himself again. Still intubated, he lay under clean sheets. She gently pulled them back to reveal his belly. It had deflated and was flat and tidy. A clean colostomy bag, with a nice pink stoma just visible through the translucent plastic, surrounded by a small fresh white bandage. There was no hint of those brief chaotic moments after the explosion.

The resident looked up at her. "I'm going to tell Dr. Gilbert what happened."

"That's why we call this a teaching hospital," she said.

Part II. FROM THE HEART

TRAUMA PATIENT #25

Your blood has forgotten your name. It seeps through hidden channels towards the abyss. Ebbs out in heavy dark torrents.

I don't know your name. Not yet. Somewhere, a clerk, seeking your driver's license, rifles through your bloody clothes. Meanwhile...

Your blood drips onto the floor where I stand, and someone puts down a blanket so I will not slip. I hold your pulse under my fingers and wait for clarity.

The whole team swirls around me, orderly but fast. We catalogue your injuries and staunch the flow. Pour a stranger's blood into your flaccid veins.

Your blood knows the forgotten secrets of your birth. Dreams, in this long night, of forgetfulness. Catches wind in its arms and lifts you to rapture.

THE NINTH LIFE

February 2

"**T**hey're going to euthanize all us aging baby boomers," I told Jonathan as we sat together over dinner at the kitchen table. "They'll sugar-coat it, offer incentives, but - you'll see."

"What?" he said, looking up from the newspaper.

"I said we're all going to be euthanized. That's how they'll solve the Medicare Social Security mess. Line us up, play nice music, off we go. The politicians. They're going to do it. Another ten years. Just wait."

"You're being silly."

"Just like the cat," I said.

"What about Pumpernickel?" He carefully folded up the newspaper and thumbed on the television. The Weather Channel.

"You keep asking me if it's time to put her to sleep. As if I know."

"You're the surgeon," he said.

I don't euthanize people, I thought. I let it lie.

I looked over to where Pumpernickel lay sprawled out on the floor by the heater vent. She was completely still.

"She's not breathing," I said. I bent over and lightly stroked one tattered ear. The ear twitched briskly, and Pumpernickel looked up and blinked at me.

"The cat's breathing, she was just sleeping," Jonathan said.

"Sorry, cat," I said.

Pumpernickel stood up with extreme deliberation. She was skeletally thin and her hair had started to come out in clumps. She had bald spots on the heels of her hind feet, and had taken to standing on his hind toes, even at rest, as if it hurt less that way. I went over and warmed a small portion of Fancy Feast in the microwave, put it down on the floor. Pumpernickel was going on 20, and her kidneys had been failing for two years.

She had been a stray kitten. When we first learned that she had kidney failure, we followed the vet's instructions precisely. We sprinkled powder on her food, and inserted pills into little Pill Pockets cunningly made from fish paste. Nights, I'd hold her pinned on the kitchen floor between my thighs, and inject her under the scruff of the neck with 150 ml of Ringer's Lactate while Jonathan monitored the injection volume. This was last autumn, when she still had her full strength.

And then, one night, as she and I fought, she turned back to look at me and I thought - why? And so I put the needles away and never did it again. She wouldn't eat the kidney failure diet, and the powder seemed to take her appetite away, so we stopped giving it to her.

She still ate the Pill Pockets - liked them better than her canned cat food, so we gave them to her for extra nutrition - but we didn't put any pills inside them. It couldn't be long. This bitterly cold winter it finally came down to watching to see if she had stopped breathing.

The kitchen was the warmest room in the house. Even so, Pumpernickel had taken to sleeping next to the heater vent under the sink. Jonathan had made a heated bed for her out of a small sheepskin dog bed lined with an electric heating pad, but the cat preferred the floor in front of the sink. So, towels were laid down and we straddled her with our feet when we stood there to wash dishes.

I was the first to awaken most mornings, and I would go downstairs half hoping that she had passed quietly in the night. Imagining the feel of a cold, rigid, body under my fingers.

For the past week, Jonathan had been talking about taking Pumpernickel for that final trip to the vet. But I prayed instead to the god of small animals for some final mercy. Peaceful passage in the night. Isn't that what we all want?

February 3

The thermometer on our back porch read 9.2 degrees when I went downstairs to get breakfast. Pumpernickel ate a few bites of cat food. Then she shook herself, staggered, and almost fell over. I walked over to her, and she rubbed against my leg and purred. I lifted her to put her back into her place in front of the sink. She barely filled my two hands, light as a small stuffed animal but not as soft, a skeleton covered by fur.

I was covering the Trauma Service that February, and I spent most of the day trying to resuscitate a teenager who had shot himself – accident or deliberate, nobody seemed to know – in the head. The entrance wound was just under his left eye, and so small that, but for the powder burns, you might miss it.

The paramedics had wrapped his head with an Ace bandage. When I unwrapped it, dark blood sluiced from an exit wound behind his right ear, a hole big enough to admit half of my fist. I stuffed the hole with gauze and held my gloved hand over it, slowing the flow but not stopping it. The bleeding was implacable – the kind that comes from the great venous sinuses that line the back of the skull. The main drain, where all the blood coming back from the brain comes together before heading south, back to the heart again.

I'd seen this once before, in the operating room, watching the neurosurgeons explore another head injured patient, and I knew this was a mortal wound. Sure, we would do our best for this youngster, call the neurosurgeons, whip the blood bank into a frenzy keeping up with our demands. But your goal shifts at a time like this. There would be no thought of a save, simply the will to keep the kid alive long enough for the parents to make it to the hospital. Maybe even work toward organ donation.

We get a lot of self-inflicted gunshot wounds in February. Mostly elderly men, living alone. Round about February, it seems like winter will never end. It's easy to feel that nothing good will ever come again, I guess, if you are all alone in a big house.

February 4

At dinner, Jonathan asked me again about Pumpernickel.

I had gone to the autopsy on the kid just before coming home from work. Hole blasted right through the *torcula herophili*, those great spaces in the back of the skull lined by venous cisterns as big as your thumb but with walls as thin as cigarette paper. There was nothing we could have done to save him. He had looked even younger, lying nude on the stainless steel table in the morgue. Tomorrow, I would have to call his folks. Talk it all through with them again. The last time we spoke, his mother told me about hearing the shot. Rushing into his room to see him lying inert, face down, on the hooked rug. The blood.

"Pumpernickel doesn't seem to be suffering," I said. "Give her time. It can't be much longer."

Jonathan turned back to his newspaper. I had a pillowcase ready to wrap the cat in. I knew where to take her for pet cremation. When the time came.

Jonathan retired from his job last year, so he was the one who cleaned up when Pumpernickel pooped on the floor. Jonathan was the one who caught Pumpernickel squatting over the heater vent in the kitchen floor, about to let loose with a stream of dilute cat pee. Not healthy urine, pungent with waste matter; but kidney failure urine, clear and odorless as water.

Entropy, was all Jonathan had said when he told me about it. The force driving the universe forward into chaos. The same word he'd used when my mother tried to nibble, gently, at the pen we'd given her to sign her durable power of attorney for health care papers.

February 5

We came back from an evening concert to find the kitchen empty. After much diligent searching, I heard a faint unshaped mewl from the darkest corner of the basement. I carried Pumpernickel upstairs into the warm kitchen, and she ate a bit of cat food. She drank thirstily, then paced very slowly around the kitchen, circling, circling, each step seeming to take great effort. Her head was bowed down and she walked as if blind, in the last extremity of fatigue. A mountaineer lost in a whiteout on Everest. The kid's mother, walking down the long corridor from the SICU for the last time.

I picked Pumpernickel up, and her head went limp on my left wrist, and I carried her back downstairs, made her a little nest from old towels and turned on a space heater. Left her there.

February 6

I dreamed that my mother was calling me from the garage, where I'd made a bed for her and then forgotten her for a month. When I opened the garage door and turned on the light, she smiled and held out her arms and my heart broke.

I decided not to look down in the basement until I'd eaten my breakfast. Halfway through my cereal, I heard a faint mewl. There she was, standing at the foot of the basement stairs. Planted defiantly and squarely on all four feet. This time, when I brought her upstairs she just stood in a daze in front of the water bowl. I smeared some cat food on my index finger and painted it thickly on her snout. She didn't lick it off. I thought I felt a faint purr as I held her, and her heart felt like a small bird's when I cupped my hand around her small rib cage.

Around noon we had a break in the trauma action, and I called Jonathan.

"How's Pumpernickel?"

"Sleeping. Last night, after you went to bed, I heard this strange thumping. I went downstairs, and she had gotten into the space under the sink. I leave it open so the pipes won't freeze, you know? She had bumbled around and pushed the cabinet drawer out from the back side. She was inside one of the drawers."

"Want me to call the vet?" I said slowly.

"She hasn't taken any water today. She's simply crawled away to die. Cats do that."

February 7

Somewhere in the early morning hours my pager went off and I was called out to help stabilize a trauma patient in the SICU. By the time we had him tucked in, it was almost 4 am. Early enough to go home for a shower and some fresh clothes, before I had to return for my 7:15 OR start time.

The house was dark and silent when I opened the door from the garage. I paused, waiting for Pumpernickel to come trotting up to rub against my leg, to beg for an early breakfast. Then I remembered. I set my mittens and keys down on the side table and went downstairs, still in my heavy parka and ski cap.

Pumpernickel lay in front of the space heater, barely visible in the shadowy moonlight. She didn't move when I touched her lightly, but when I cradled my hands around her ribcage I still felt the fast butterfly wing pulse of her heartbeat. I gently settled her down onto the towels and moved the space heater closer.

I sat in the dark kitchen and sipped a cup of coffee. Walked softly upstairs into our bedroom, took off my clothes. As I slipped gently into bed, I reached out to enfold Jonathan, and felt him turn toward me in the dark.

BY THE BOOK

"I don't shake hands anymore," Julia says, as I hold out my right hand. This is the year of swine flu, or H1N1 as we've been asked to call it here in the Midwest. She's right, of course, the handshake is passé, a way of sharing germs rather than a friendly gesture. But, somehow the alternative fist bump or elbow tap doesn't just seem to convey what my handshake used to. She sits on the exam table, writing tablet in her right hand, pen in her left. I steal a glance at the tablet as I pull back my hand. As usual, she has a list.

Taken by surprise, I do the only thing that comes to mind. I steeple the fingertips of my right hand with my left, press my palms together in front of my chest, and bow slightly. I stop just short of saying, "Namaste."

I was raised Methodist and I'm pretty sure Julia grew up Catholic, but we are both children of the world. The gesture evidently resonates, because she smiles and, setting down pen and paper, salutes me in return. I turn to her husband, and repeat my overture.

I've been taking care of Julia for about eight years now. I'm her surgeon, and it all started here in my office. A familiar story. Doctor, I've found a lump in my breast. The biopsy. The news. The mastectomy. Adjuvant chemotherapy. A pause to catch our breath, a hope, and then two years later, persistent pain in her back. The bone scan. Radiation. Three years later, blinding headaches. A brain metastasis. Stereotaxic radiosurgery. Radiation-induced cataracts. Weight loss. Quality of life. And, for the past two years, mets scattered like snowflakes throughout her chest on x-ray. Miraculously stable. Her Living Will, carefully filled out and filed away, mercifully not needed, not yet.

"This is Jeremy, our medical student," I say. "Is it okay with you if he sits in today?" She nods graciously, and then we both ignore him. Our gazes, hers and mine, are locked. I'm always amazed when this happens. The extras, the medical or nursing students, the potential intruders – they just disappear. It has been six months since I last saw her.

"I refused to have that mammogram again," she says. "I hope that's okay with you." We're at the end of the morning session of clinic, lunch is over due, and so I've simply dragged Jeremy into this exam room without any preamble. No summarized history, no chance to clue him in. No time for the Socratic method, not if we both want to grab a quick bite to eat before afternoon clinic starts.

Julia is swathed in one of our Breast Clinic ponchos. The flowers have faded to obscurity through too many washings. She's looking good – her eyes are clear, and she even has a thin layer of subcutaneous fat. She's never weighed more than 130 pounds, and during the worst of the chemotherapy she had to be hospitalized twice. Twice, I've thought she was going to die. She goes on, "I had cataract surgery."

Her husband adds, "She's sketching again, for the first time in years. Working on a new series of drawings."

"You look great," I say, stalling for time as I page through her electronic chart. Her last mammogram, on her remaining breast, was two years ago. A small shadow, BIRADS 4a, probably benign. The radiologist had recommended a six month return. She's definitely overdue. Who ordered that damned mammogram, two years ago, anyhow? It looks like I did.

"I feel great. I'm finally starting to feel good. I can see again. It's like the lights went on."

I nod as I make a few notes. Thanks to my dead mother, who made me take a typing class in high school, I can document in her chart and maintain eye contact with her at the same time. It slows the pace of the encounter, lets me get my ducks in a row. Normally she would simply be followed by her medical oncologist at this point. Metastatic carcinoma. There isn't much I, her surgeon, can do for her. But we've seen each other every six months for so long... once I tried to lengthen it to a year, but she protested.

We go through the usual questions. Any lumps? No. Any problems with the surgical site? No. The arm? Nipple discharge – from the other breast, I mean? Pain anywhere? Cough? No, no, and no, on through the whole list. Her voice grows raspy and her husband passes her a water bottle. Among other side effects, she now suffers from a lack of saliva. She takes a long swig and hands it back to him. Her weight is up six pounds, and we're both ecstatic about this.

I get up from the small desk and go to the small sink, wash my hands. She hands her pen and tablet over to her husband as I approach, and takes off her cape to fully bare her torso. Most other patients, I am the one to lift up the cape, but this is Julia and we've been through a lot together. I scrutinize her chest. The nicely healed obliquely oriented mastectomy incision. Pectoral muscle, ribs, I can even see her heart beat through the scant amount of tissue that is left. The other breast looks normal. I run through the exam and, mercifully, find nothing amiss.

So, what about that mammogram? She's definitely at increased risk. Personal history of breast cancer. Family history of breast cancer. And, an abnormal mammogram two years ago with no follow up. The American Cancer Society would say that early detection saves lives. What if there is a tiny new cancer hidden there? Another biopsy. Another mastectomy. More chemotherapy. I have a junior partner fresh out of fellowship. He'd know what to do. "I always follow the established protocol, if there is one," is how he cuts to the heart of any complex problem at our Tumor Board.

Jeremy hasn't moved. He knows the right answer. Go by the book. Talk her into it. Make her have the study. After all, she *could* have another cancer. Isn't this why she's in Breast Clinic, so I can check the opposite breast? We'll have to debrief after this encounter.

I go through her list. The big question – how long do I have? – is never asked.

And the mammogram? Well, this is the third time we've struggled with that decision together. Does that make it easier? Surely she would have lump by now... On the other hand, if there *is* something there, I'm giving it more time to grow, to spread, to metastasize...

I say slowly, "I don't feel anything in that breast. You're doing very well, by all accounts. Let's just check you again in six months. If you feel anything, or anything changes, you call me and we'll get you in right away."

"Doctor Beth, I love you," she says. "I shouldn't call you Doctor Beth, but that's how I think of you." In that instant, I realize that she would go for the mammogram, if I told her to, and I almost change my mind.

"I love it," I say. "Six months. Call me if anything changes." I rise, press my hands together, bow to her.

"Namaste," she says. It means – the Spirit in me recognizes the Spirit in you. Or, sometimes, simply, long life. "Maybe we'll start a trend," she adds.

"Namaste, Julia."

EVENING ROUNDS

I still needed to make evening rounds. Just one week earlier, I had been home recovering from a sudden illness. My body had served me well for 58 years, and so it had been a shock to find myself in a bed on the cardiac unit, being treated for an irregular heart beat. I was discharged on four medications – so easily we cross the line from health into illness – and I still felt off kilter, as if waiting for the next physical betrayal.

I'm a cancer surgeon. My cardiologist had cleared me to return to work the week before, but this was the first day I had scheduled a full list of cases in the operating room. Now the simple pleasure of once again immersing myself in surgery had given way to profound fatigue. I was simultaneously eager to get home to my own husband, yet loathe to leave the warmth of my office for the sleet-filled November night outside.

I cupped my mug of decaf in my hands for a moment, then drank the dregs and stood up uncertainly. Time for rounds. I could, of course, simply call the resident of the night and make sure all the patients were okay. Pack up my briefcase, lock my office, and be home in twenty minutes. But that would have required conscious thought. I was so tired that, instead, out of habit, I plodded down the hallway toward the part of the sprawling academic medical center where the surgical patients were housed.

As I rounded the last corner into the main lobby, I began to hear music. There, next to the large ficus trees, a choir was singing "Amazing Grace". "'Twas Grace that taught my heart to fear..." Eyes closed, I leaned against the wall and listened with the throng of staff, visitors, and patients.

"Was blind, but now I see."

When I was discharged from the hospital, I had asked my cardiologist what lay ahead. His reply – "I hesitate to predict the future" – shadowed a future that had previously seemed limitless. I patted the left-hand pocket of my white coat to assure myself that the vial of pills was still there, in case my heart danced a tarantella again.

* * *

It was after 7:00 when I got to the last patient. A routine postop check on my second surgical case of the day. The surgery, a right hemicolectomy for cancer, had gone smoothly, with minimal blood loss. A quick look at the dressings, pulse and blood pressure, and a brief reassurance to a patient still groggy from anesthesia, and move on. But when I entered the room I was surprised to see my patient, Jane Malloy, sitting up. The TV on the opposite wall was tuned to CNN with closed captioning. This particular patient was a visually-impaired deaf mute woman who made and sold earthenware pottery in several of our local galleries. One of her mugs, striped with ochre taken from deep-sea mud cores, held pencils on my desk. The sign-language interpreter had left for the evening.

Jane's posture was regal, and her gaze alert. Her lightly-flowered dressing gown was drawn up high and neatly buttoned. As I hesitated on the doorstep, she set down the small assistive lens through which she had been watching television, glanced in my direction and seemed to recognize me. I wondered just how much vision she actually had. Probably, perceiving people only as moving shapes, she had learned to recognize them by subtle differences in movement, sound, scent, the very texture of an individual, that were lost on those with normal vision.

Jane sat up even straighter, and waved me closer. As was her habit, she seemed to held my gaze with her eyes for a long moment – I knew she wasn't really looking into my eyes, but still it was unsettling – and then reached for a battered spiral-bound notebook and felt-tipped calligrapher's pen. Holding the notebook in her left hand, she anchored it securely against her forehead and nose. She brought up the pen and wrote on a line held two inches from her right eye, sliding the notebook from side to side to keep the tip of her pen within a narrow field of vision.

I sat down heavily on the foot of the bed and waited. Thought about dinner. This was not going to be a quickie. Jane held out the notebook and pen in my general direction and I took them. I turned the notebook around and read:

"What did you find?"

I was astonished by the question; how alert could she be, just four or five hours since surgery? I uncapped the felt tip-pen and wrote in careful block printing:

"We were able to get the tumor out, but I felt some spots on your liver and took a biopsy." Few patients were so lucid this soon after surgery. I realized that these words would not be lost in some post-anesthesia fog. I imagined Jane reading and re-reading what I wrote over the long night ahead, and even into the next week and farther. Choosing my words with care, I wrote:

"The biopsy showed tumor. We did a frozen section."

I passed it back to Jane, who scanned the page closely and wrote:

"Were you able to remove it?"

"It was many small nodules, each no bigger than a fingertip. Not something I could cut out. But there are other treatments we can use." Jane had very long thin fine fingers, I noticed for the first time. The nails were cut square across. I wondered if she cut them by feel, or if she held each one up to her good right eye to check it out as she filed it with an emery board. I wrote further.

"You will need chemotherapy after you recover from the surgery."

Scritch, scritch. How could a felt-tip pen could make so much noise? Outside, it was dark. The patient wrote intently, in a frenzy. I relaxed, took a few deep breaths. Except for the noise of the pen, the room was unusually still. I relaxed even further into the quiet. It was good to sit still, the weight of my body off my feet again. Noise from the nurse's station outside intruded periodically.

The surgical resident on call caught my eye from the doorway. I nodded, and he glided into the room and sat on the other corner of the foot of the bed. Ignoring the interruption, Jane continued to write.

"I'm telling her what we found," I said softly, as if the patient could hear and a loud word could break the mood.

We read the next few sentences together, heads almost touching over the notebook.

"What kind of chemotherapy? Will you still be my doctor? Will I have to stay in the hospital the whole time?"

Each question deserved a paragraph, maybe a page, and I was so tired...squaring my shoulders, I picked up the pen and wrote, *"The usual chemotherapy is given intravenously and most people tolerate it well."* It didn't always work particularly well, either, I knew, but this wasn't the time for the complete brutal truth. I found that I chose my words with great care - somehow, writing was so permanent - but at the same time I had to fight the tendency to lapse into a kind of pidgin, as if Jane were retarded or foreign as well as visually handicapped.

I wrote about a paragraph and moved on to #2. *"I will be your doctor for as long as you need me. Another Dr will manage your chemo, but I will be right there with you all the way."*

Two down, on to #3. *"You will be able to go home as soon as you have recovered from surgery - probably about a week from now. You do not have to be in the hospital to get chemotherapy."*

I passed it back and watched Jane scan it past her good eye, stabilizing the notebook against her forehead and nose as before and nodding from time to time as she read.

The resident asked softly, "What does she have around her neck?"

"It's called an optical assistive device. It's like a miniature telescope. She was using it to watch TV when I came in."

"She has a beautiful handwriting." And indeed she did, a kind of fine italic semi-printing, which used the chiseled end of a two-ended calligraphic black felt-tipped pen to good effect. Jane's choice of words was also striking – had she been to college? At what point in childhood had she become disabled? I realized that I had never bothered to ask.

She was again writing busily. A blanket of peace settled over the room. The resident said softly, "It makes you realize how lucky..." the rest left unsaid.

Jane passed the notebook again and the resident and I read, *"And you, doctor, how are you doing? Are you well?"* I stopped breathing. Had she known that I had been sick? How had she known? Was she one of the patients in clinic that day when I, stricken, had to walk away from my duty and seek care in the emergency room of my own hospital? Had her surgery been rescheduled, delayed because of my own needs? Or was this just a polite inquiry? The resident froze, barely breathing.

Doctors are not supposed to get sick. And if we do get sick, we pretend it never happened. Some of us seek treatment in distant cities, just to protect that façade, returning a bit thinner and paler from an extended "vacation". Others, like me, want desperately to be in the care of colleagues, in the familiar environment in which we spend the majority of our waking hours. Even so, once we are back at work, everybody politely pretends nothing has happened.

I dropped the pen, stalling for time as I chased it under her bed. I uncapped it, looked at the resident. I started to write *"I'm fine, thanks,"* and then crossed it out. Wrote, *"It's been a long day,"* and crossed it out. Slowly and carefully I wrote, *"I have been sick myself recently, with a minor heart problem. But now I am feeling much better. My doctor says things look very good for now."* I paused and added, *"Thank you for asking."*

Jane looked at me with those unfathomable eyes and nodded slightly. She reached out her hand and I grasped it. Her hand was warm, the fingers strong and callused from molding wet clay. We stared at each other through another long pause. The resident remained frozen. Jane gave my fingers a tiny squeeze, let go, and then wrote one last paragraph.

I read, *"When I told my Pastor that I had cancer, he said, Do not worry about the future, God is already there. Thank you for taking the time to explain things to me."*

I handed the notebook to the resident, who read the last lines and passed it back to Janet. Then the resident and I got up and walked gently out of the room. My heart pumped slowly and surely in my chest.

FROM THE HEART

A woman sits in the examining room, clutching a flow-ered poncho about her slender frame. Husband sits on a chair next to her. If you met her at a cocktail party, she would be the elegant one wearing the deceptively simple gown and understated jewelry. Now she looks hollowed out. The color has left her face. I'm suddenly conscious of the small sounds beyond this quiet room. Nurses' voices, something brushing against the closed door. Her gaze never wavers from my eyes. Her name is Sharon.

Sharon's mammograms hang on the x-ray view box. An irregular shadow, opaque white against the cobwebby grey of normal tissue, can be seen from where I sit at the small desk. The radiologist has done a needle biopsy. I, her surgeon, have just had to tell her that it's cancer.

I've eased into it as best I know how. Started with neutral words like "shadow" or "opacity" and then becoming more spe-cific. "Growth", "tumor", "cancer". I've tried to emphasize the positives. Now I repeat myself, hoping she hears me.

"It's only about the size of the tip of my finger," I say, reaching up and demonstrating. "Your exam is normal. It's excellent that you've been getting routine mammograms. You have a really good chance of a cure."

Tears well. These rooms are stocked with boxes of tissues, and now I hand her one. Her husband draws his chair closer to hers. I busy myself with her chart, give them a moment to absorb what I have just said.

* * *

It's six months earlier. I'm lying on a stretcher in the emergency room of this same hospital. My heart pummels the inside of my chest with a new, erratic rhythm. The ER doctor has just told me I have atrial fibrillation. She's admitting me to the cardiac unit.

My physician husband sits on a chair on the other side of the gurney. We all know what this means. I muster enough breath to protest, saying, "But I've always been so active. I've never been sick. I bike to work, eat right…" I'm looking into her eyes. I'm drowning, I can't breathe, she's grasped my hand, she'll pull me out.

"All of that will stand you in good stead," she says calmly.

* * *

Ten days later, Sharon lies on the operating table. I stand at her right side, looking down into those eyes, holding her hand. I'm going to do a breast-conserving operation. She won't lose her breast, not today. The Anesthesiologist puts a mask on her face. "This is just oxygen," he says.

"You're going to go to sleep now. You may feel some warmth in your arm, that's just the medicine," I say. I speak softly, slowly, my gestures deliberately calmed to gentle her. Inside, I'm as keyed up as a violinist awaiting the conductor's baton.

A milky white liquid flows into her intravenous line. Propofol, "milk of amnesia", bringing instant unconsciousness and forgetfulness. She moves slightly. The drug always burns a bit as it goes in. Within a couple of seconds, she grows still. I place her hand carefully on the armboard, secure it in place so that I can work. So I can remove the lump, test the lymph nodes. Once she is asleep, things move swiftly.

* * *

A cardiac nurse glides in and out of my darkened room that first night, always increasing the drip flowing into my right arm. It's not working. My pulse dances chaotically, tracing an erratic line across the monitor. They will have to shock my heart.

In the morning, the senior cardiologist prepares to do the cardioversion. He checks the equipment, the EKG leads, the paddles. He stands at the head of my bed, his strong fingers hooked under my jaw, holding the clear plastic mask over my nose and mouth. Deep breaths. I'm so tired.

"It's just oxygen," he says. A nurse pushes propofol into my I.V. "Tell me what you did on vacation," the cardiologist says. The drug warms my right arm. Good. "We went kayaking…" I start to say.

* * *

Two months later, Sharon is in the middle of chemotherapy. Her hair is falling out, so she shaved her head. Her husband shaved his in sympathy, and so did his buddies at work. Her breast has healed well. The cosmetic result is excellent. When she finishes chemo, she will undergo radiation treatment.

"I used to run three miles every day," she says. "Now I walk. When I can. I get so tired."

"Your body is telling you to conserve your strength. You'll run again. When this is all behind you," her husband says. I nod.

"Just do what you can, for now. Give yourself a couple of months. It will be a bit like training for your first 5K run. You'll have to build back up, but it will come," I say.

"I ran my first 5K in 41 minutes. I finished dead last," she says. Laughs.

And then stops, as if surprised by the sound of her own laughter.

* * *

I go home from the hospital on five medications. Meds to slow my heartbeat, to regulate it, to lower my blood pressure, to thin my blood. My heart won't beat faster than 60, except when it reverts to its hectic, danse macabre. Leaves begin to fall.

In our garage, dusty spider webs enshroud my bicycle. Every day after work, I trudge around the track at the student center, clutching the handrail for steadiness. I seem to have aged ten years. Early winter snow will fly before I jog again. Scout's pace at first. Jog 20 steps, walk 20, repeat, repeat, repeat. Slowly, tentatively, starting all over from the bottom. And, in due course, I go into a kind of remission. The meds are reduced, and then all but two of them are dropped.

* * *

Sharon continues, "I just don't understand why I got breast cancer. Nobody in my family ever had it. I never smoked. I've eaten right, exercised, kept to my ideal weight…"

This would be a good time to tell her about the research - scientists all over the world, trying to ferret out that very issue. But I've been a surgeon for thirty five years, and the answers remain elusive.

Or maybe I should share my own story with her. Tell her how I got back into my life again after being sick. But we are in Sharon's story, not mine.

So I just speak from the heart.

"It's a rotten disease. It just strikes anyone it pleases. You didn't do anything wrong," I say. "You will get over this and get your life back. And, as for those good habits, all that will stand you in good stead."

JOSHUA AND THE PIG

China. October 1992.

J oshua is a small gray gnome of a surgeon. Deep-set eyes under thick gray eyebrows peer shrewdly at a world that has sometimes treated him harshly. He is a citizen of the world. He left his birthplace in Eastern Europe long ago and with few regrets. He is an odd mix of California (his adopted homeland) and Bucharest (his birthplace). His vocabulary is pure Angelino spiced with Yiddish. When an operation goes well, he pauses to say "mahh-vell-ous!" – savoring the word and the moment, making the sound long and drawn out.

We are a group of five surgeons, sent to China to teach laparoscopic surgery in Shanghai and Beijing. He is our leader. By the end of the trip, the Chinese surgeons in those two cities have learned more than just laparoscopic surgery – they now say "mahh-vell-ous" with almost the same intonation.

When we are told it is impossible for us to make rounds, to see the patients our team will be operating upon before and after surgery, it is Joshua who takes the chief surgeon aside and straightens things out. Joshua and the chief surgeon return from their huddle, and Joshua nods to me and says softly, "Beth, there is always a way."

Winter is rapidly settling over China. Skies are gray, and it is dark and cold inside the hospitals where we work as well as outside. It is too early to waste power by turning on the light or the heat. We wear sweatshirts under our scrub suits, except when we are actually performing surgery. Indeed, China is bleak and dark, forbidding, just starting to open up to the West. The Beijing air is harsh and biting with sulfur dioxide, soot, and other pollutants. Our Chinese guide says, "We have three problems in China: population, power, and pollution."

I am the only female surgeon on the team. Every day, I change my clothes in the women's locker room. The floors are wet and gritty, and the air is fetid from the squat toilet in its stall. But the air is warmly moist with steam, and fragrant as well, because the nurses shower and wash their clothes here. Every day, someone places a clean scrub suit, socks, and immaculate white operating room sneakers in my locker.

The operating rooms have large windows to admit the wintry gray light. The equipment is excellently maintained, the physicians well-trained.

After each day lecturing and operating, we ride back to our hotel in silence in a converted school bus. The streets are dark, most cars and buses don't waste gasoline on headlights. The occasional headlights are glow sullenly yellow with reduced wattage.

About every city block, a single faint golden light bulb hangs in front of a small shop or restaurant. People cluster in these islands of light; we see a man cutting hair under one light, a woman selling vegetables under another, and racks of clothes displayed under the next one. The walled groups of houses beyond are all dark. We stand under hot showers in our hotel rooms, and lather ourselves lavishly with soap, before layering up to go out to dinner with our hosts. The food is wondrous and mysterious.

At home, we each have positions of power and influence, but none more so than Joshua. He is a true pioneer, one of the first to adopt laparoscopic surgery to common surgical problems, extolling the virtues of this surgical technique long before any others. We are professors, each in our own hospital, but only Joshua is both professor *and* Chief of Surgery.

Bundled in a thick gray quilted coat, Joshua stands heavily rooted to the ground. He barely comes up to my armpit, sometimes dozes at the supper-table, and pops his heart pills whenever he thinks no one is watching. As the trip progresses he becomes both elder statesman and cultural translator. Not that he speaks Chinese, or has been to China before (he hasn't), but rather that he understands the communists. He knows what it is like after the revolution.

In China, he remembers other days in other countries. The sharp eyes become clouded at times. He looks sad. He makes remarks like, "But, of course, that is what happens during a revolution." He nods his head, empathizing with our frustratingly oblique Chinese guide. "She cannot tell us that because, of course, she has not been given that information. That is how it is."

He alone is not surprised when we find that *USA-Today* is not obtainable in Beijing. He assumes the phones are tapped, and it doesn't particularly bother him. He simply says, "Folks, you have no *idee*..." when we find it unfathomable that the hotel dining room closes at 7 pm. Joshua probably *always* assumes the phone is tapped, the room bugged, the restaurant closed.

In China we sleep with our passports stashed in small cloth bags close to our hearts. But I suspect that even in California

Joshua is never without his passport. He may even keep a stash of gold or diamonds somewhere handy, hidden near the back door perhaps, in case of emergencies. What kind of emergencies? The knock on the door after midnight. Or, perhaps, another revolution. After all, America has already had one, not to mention the Civil War, a failed revolution of sorts.

"How many revolutions have you lived through, Joshua?"

Silence. He has to count.

"Three. Or, maybe four. But maybe the fourth one doesn't count."

The rest of us, four US-born surgeons who have never seen even a single revolution, think this one through. How could a revolution *not* count? All four of us, even me, tower over Joshua. Our parents knew no shortage of food, and stuffed us with vitamins as we were growing. You could put two of Joshua inside any one of us. Joshua, in contrast, was conceived and grown during times of famine. He feels right at home here where some things are unaccountably unobtainable and other things are abundant and cheap. That is how it is under the communists.

When we are taken to see the sights, Joshua refuses to go into the Great Hall of the People. "I've seen it before," he says, and he doesn't mean in Beijing. He sits down on a stone wall outside the entrance, and settles into his overcoat to wait for the rest of us. His collar almost meets the brim of his fur lined cap.

Toward the end of our last week in China, Joshua's elegant and cosmopolitan wife organizes a farewell banquet. It is a festive affair, held in the basement of a restaurant she has found that serves Western style food. The food is actually sort of a Beijing interpretation of French cuisine. French food filtered through an Eastern consciousness. There is a Karaoke setup. There is wine, singing, and much talk. We have all enjoyed the trip, but now we are eager to get home. Joshua picks at his food. The bushy eyebrows hood his dark eyes. While the rest of us trade stories about our experiences in China, he alone is silent. I nudge him.

"A penny for your thoughts."

He looks at me.

"I was thinking about my pig."

"Joshua, don't tell me you are keeping pigs in LA? You must be the only laparoscopic surgeon on the staff of University Hospital who has his own pig!"

"No, Beth. Not now. Many years ago. When I was in school, back home, I had a pig. You understand, this was strictly forbidden. No one could own anything, much less an animal. But there is always a way. I had a pig. A farmer gave it to me in exchange for some old clothes I had outgrown. The clothes he needed for his own son, who was a few years younger than I. Another farmer, ten kilometers from my town, kept the pig for me. People saved scraps of food for it. This too was forbidden. Everyone who helped, you understand, had a share in the pig."

He pauses for a drink of wine. This is a long speech for Joshua. I have just enough time to wonder – a pig? Isn't Joshua Jewish?

Then he goes on, "Every night, after dark, I schlepped around. I'd collect my bucket of scraps, and bicycle out to feed my pig. The number of people entitled to a share in my pig kept growing and growing. Even the local authorities in the village had a share. So they would look the other way, you understand. But the pig grew also.

"Finally we slaughtered it and cooked it. The man who butchered the pig got a piece. The night watchman got a piece, so he would ignore the sounds the pig made when we killed it. Everyone got a piece. But there was still plenty. It was a good pig. There is always a way, you see."

INUNDATION

Friday, July second, 6 pm, and I was on Trauma call. The hospital swarmed with new residents; an army of interns who had been medical students a few weeks back, of second year residents who had been interns just two days ago, and, at the top of the heap, the fresh chief residents – my surgical chiefs, and the medicine chiefs, and the OB-GYN chiefs, pediatrics....

All over the hospital attending faculty physicians like me shifted uneasily, as if feeling the angel of Death hover just outside like some sick imitation of a MedEvac chopper – those great dark wings beating time with one's heartbeat. I shivered and thought, *there is no angel of Death. Maybe it will be a quiet night.*

This July was different. Our town was in the grips of a slow-motion flood. Under normal circumstances, our little river flowed in a predictable fashion through the middle of town, lazy and pea green, or hurried and brown, its flow modulated by a flood control reservoir. This year the waters, fed by an extraordinary conjunction of heavy snows and torrential spring rains over the entire reservoir catchment area, had breached the spillway. Uncontrolled, the river crept about one foot higher every day. The normal sense of isolation that set in on the night shift was amplified beyond reason. Not many would be celebrating this July fourth.

The town split into two separate communities as the bridges across the river shut down, one by one. About ten days ago, we had been directed to decide which side of the river we wanted to be on, to go to that side, and to stay there. For those of us who worked at the hospital, there was no decision. We were directed to spend the duration of the flood on the hospital side of the river. I was fortunate enough to live on that same side of town. For the rest, there were makeshift dormitories.

One of the major hospitals in an adjoining city had just been forced to close when water gained access to the basement, where the blood bank, power plant, and information technology services were housed. Patients that would have gone to that hospital now came to ours. The slow pace of the flood gave time for armies of volunteers to sand bag. Watching it play out in slow motion was excruciating.

I found myself uneasy at some profound visceral level. Fear of being lost, fear of separation from my husband. Spending this night away from him was worrisome, even though we lived on high ground, even though there was no threat whatsoever to us. I felt as spooked as a frightened horse.

The river crept up so slowly that you would have to watch it for a couple of hours to see a change. Every day more rain fell, adding to the misery of those fighting the water, and swelled the flood ever higher. It was already well past the hundred-year flood plane.

As the waters rose, animals, displaced by the flood, appeared in more populated parts of town. The town had always had a large resident deer population, but now the deer were joined by coyotes, skunks, snakes, raccoons. Supercell thunderstorms popped up from nowhere, fueled by unseasonably hot temperatures. Such storms could dump an inch or so of rain in an hour before moving on. Dumpsters floated in the river and lodged against the bridges.

I resolutely put the flood out of my mind and pulled out the student-run daily newspaper to check the TV listings. The local stations were running flood coverage 24/7. The town was under a mandatory curfew until 5 am. I settled into the call room for the night. There was a Star Trek rerun at 9 pm. *Check some news, get some dinner, prowl the ER/ICU/wards, and maybe work on that manuscript while waiting for something bad to happen. Get up to the call room in time for the Star Trek…careful, old girl, don't jinx yourself. Tonight of all nights. Hot July, new residents….*

I wanted to call home, to hear the calm voice of my husband, but the phone lines to our outlying development had been down for the past 24 hours. Cell phone service was out as well. I turned on the television instead. The cable had gone out; nothing but static on our three local channels. I turned it off again. The local radio station, on low ground south of town, had gone off the air the day before.

I didn't have long to wait before the first emergency call came in on the trauma pager. 86 year old female, fell one to two stories, coming from Greenfield. CT scan at Saint Mary's Hospital. ETA 15 minutes. I quickly saved and closed out the file I'd been working on and logged off the computer. Made myself a cup of decaf coffee and shucked my clothes in the tiny bathroom, slipping into clean scrubs, warm knee-high Ragg socks and my OR clogs.

I ran into Anesthesia on the way to the ER, and we exchanged the standard pleasantries of this July – "Are you on high ground? Are you OK?"

"We're fine. You?" When I nodded, he continued, "You must be going the same place I am. She's supposed to be already intubated, but you never know." The Anesthesia resident was an upper-level. I'd worked with him before. I relaxed a notch. One less problem to worry about.

"Do you know anything about that house fire?" he asked.

"What house fire?"

"Supposed to be a bad one. North end of town, somewhere past Carlisle Avenue."

I suppressed a shiver. That was our neighborhood. All I said was, "Nope. Maybe the EMT's will know something."

We got there before the patient, which was ideal, and I went to the ambulance bay and scanned the horizon. I couldn't remember if the entrance faced north or not. I couldn't see anything, so I came back inside settled into a corner to wait. Jenny Kim, Doctor Kim now, had already started filling out the paperwork. Three pagers weighted down the waistband of her scrub pants, threatening to pull them down. Her slender hips barely held them up. Trina, the ER nurse, looked up from her own paperwork, "All you need is one more pager and you'll be Batgirl."

Commotion from the hallway. Voices, "Sailing, sailing..."

"Incoming!" someone said.

"Here they come!"

"What happened?" I asked the flight nurses.

"Fell downstairs. One or two flights. Evidently had a toddy or two. Husband's on his way, basically someone's gonna have to interpret for him, just totally stunned, poor guy. Got a cell phone number if you need it. If you can get even through on the cell phone."

"No thanks, all we need is another trauma, elderly husband in a car wreck trying to answer his cell phone and drive at the same time. Do you know anything about a house fire, north end of town?"

"We saw the flames as we approached. Looks like a hot one. Just when you need the rain, it stops."

The patient, a frail white haired woman, lay swaddled in a burrito of quilted wraps despite the July heat. The EMT's had strapped her to a long spine board and put her in a rigid cervical collar, to protect her from spinal cord damage if her back or neck were broken. Her dazed pale blue eyes, rimmed with nearly invisible lashes, wandered aimlessly around the room.

"Elsie, Elsie, squeeze my hand. Squeeze my hand...Good. This tube will help you breathe, sweetie."

"This scar is an old hiatal hernia repair. She needs an NG tube."

"Make it an OG. She's a head trauma." *Good thinking. Wouldn't want the tube going through a fractured nasal bone into the substance of the brain. Been known to happen*

The intermediate resident handed a gastric tube to the med student. "It's all yours. We'll get her off the board in a minute. Go ahead and slip it down...Advance it a little more, that's good, that's good, now put it to suction."

"Anybody check her eyes?"

"I did, 3mm reactive." The senior resident answered. His eyes were dilated, nostrils flared, he was in full alert. He had a green and yellow cloth surgical cap on – it read Nothing Runs Like a Deere. *John Deere, the local firm. It's hard to root for the local firms when they insist on cutting such wicked deals on insurance reimbursement.*

"She's got some subarachnoid blood and a frontal contusion," the Neurosurgery resident commented, over in the corner, looking at the outside head CT.

"Elsie, Elsie, do you hurt anywhere right now? Elsie?" Jenny bent over, yelled in the old woman's ear. "Squeeze my hand, Elsie, squeeze my hand, good girl."

The room was crowded. Three general surgery residents, one neurosurgery resident, one medical student, Trina and an older male ER nurse. Anesthesia was leaving – the patient was already intubated. I elbowed my way in closer. Caught the senior resident's eye. It was Bob Huber. I hadn't worked with him in almost a year, but he had gotten a reputation for solid, consistently excellent performance.

"I think this blood's all coming from the eyebrow lac. Running down. She doesn't seem to have any other obvious injuries. The head injury is the main thing. So the next step is another head CT. Might as well do chest and abdomen, get a CT of her cervical spine as well." Then, to his team, "It's July, babies, slow down and do it right. It's another July in Paradise."

"CT Tech's on the way in," said Trina.

"Right, so let's get a chest and pelvis views before we take her over."

The medical student struggled to put the Foley catheter in. Three heads converged over the target area. Bob bounced up and down on his heels, a big cat, ready to move.

"Elsie, relax, we're just doing a little procedure here." Urine flowed in the tubing. *Clear, no blood in the urine. A good sign.*

"Scanner's warming up, you can take her over anytime," Jenny reported.

Outside the door, I ran into the night EKG technician. It was one of our medical students, dressed in scrubs with a color-coordinated fanny pack sticking out of the front of his short white coat. "Hi, Jeremy, you're an EKG technician too?"

"Yup. I'm wearing my EKG hat tonight. Most of us that do these night jobs are students."

"I was a night blood gas technician when I was a student."

"Same thing, except we don't stick anyone. It's been crazy. The day student got called to the ER eight times, I've already been called down five times...Hey, Dr Abernathy, I'm thinking of going into surgery. Can I come by and talk with you sometime?"

"You bet. Be my pleasure."

Jeremy smiled and nodded, dashed away with his little cart.

"Hope you have your running shoes on," I said softly. The emergency medicine resident came down the hall toward me. "Hey, you know anything about a house fire? North end of town?"

"Nope, but it wouldn't surprise me. That's all we need."

I stuck my head back into the Trauma room. Looked at the monitor – BP holding steady, abdomen soft, looked like they could handle it for a while. "Call me if you need me, and let me know what those x-rays show."

I tried to call home. Phone lines were still out, so I went up on the hospital roof, stood next to the helicopter, and looked out toward the north. Flames somewhere on the horizon, just to the left of the water tower. I tried to make out landmarks, get my bearings, but it was just trees and the aging water tower.

Once, I had ridden the helicopter to a multiple casualty situation to the north of town. We had circled the pad and taken the mandatory noise-reduction flight path out until we were far enough and high enough to head north. We had passed the water tower, and then flown over my neighborhood. Had we passed to the left of the water tower or to the right? Which way? I couldn't remember.

Chances were, we were fine. But my unease had nothing to do with logic. I wanted to get on my bike in the dark and head home, to see for myself. Stupid. Couldn't abandon my post.

I went back downstairs and settled uneasily back in the call room with my cup of decaf, put my feet up on the bed, and waited. I thought back over my trek to the hospital, about how impossible it would be to bike home in the dark, despite my halogen headlights.

That morning, the street I normally took to get to the hospital had been closed. The bridge which fed that street had been shut down. I stood for a few minutes and watched as engineers checked the subsurface for scour around the piers, walking up and down with long poles.

Holes had been drilled through the road surface of the bridge to relieve the pressure of trapped air and rising water. To prevent the bridge from simply lifting up and floating away. The underside of that bridge had been studded with swallow's nests, I recalled, and now I wondered were the swallows had gone.

Swallows, flitting over the river in the early morning sun as I biked in... Swallows returning every year...swallows making little mud nests...

I must have fallen asleep, because I awoke with a jerk when the pager went off again in a half hour. It was Bob. "There's a stab wound coming in from Lone Tree."

"Who's your chief resident?" I asked him.

Silence. "Uh, I'm a chief."

Oops, I thought, right. *As of this week. You are indeed.* "Sorry, Bob."

Bob continued, "He was in a bar fight. He was holding a knife and he fell on it accidentally. Stabbed himself in the right upper quadrant."

"And you believe this?"

"I just report what I'm told. He's coming via chopper. They had to borrow a chopper, MedEvac's out on a neonatal run. ETA's less than five minutes."

"I'll meet you down there."

Bob and I checked the Trauma room. The nurses' aide ran back and forth, restocking the room. The old lady was over in the scanner.

"Cold in here. We need the heater on."

Anesthesia returned. "Nice to see you again. OR busy?"

"Very."

"What about that colectomy?"

"We were just about to send for it. Now it's on hold for this."

Bob and I found an empty gurney, sat on it, feet up on the collapsed side rail, knees up. The med student joined us. *We're the three monkeys - hear no evil, see no evil, speak no evil.*

"So now it seems a bit worse. His belly's getting bigger, according to the patient and the flight nurse," I said to the medical student, to break the silence.

"So I guess we'll do the FAST and if it's positive, we'll go up to the OR."

"OR's been notified," Bob noted.

"OR's backed up."

"Doesn't matter. Trauma trumps everything. We go to the head of the line and they have the staff to handle it. That's what makes us a Level I trauma center."

Silence again. And then, "Say, Dr Abernathy, I've been wondering... I hope you don't mind me asking..."

"Go ahead, spit it out."

"Why do you still take Trauma call? Most Department Chairs don't."

"Do you have any idea how many meetings a Chair has to go to? Or how dull they are? You wanna be a Chair yourself someday?"

Heads shook with an emphatic no all around.

I continued, "The really fun part is teaching and operating. All the rest is just work. Besides, I'm not gonna leave you guys alone. Every time I turn my back, you come up with another trauma." I went over to the outside corridor and looked out the window. No glow on the horizon. They must have gotten the fire under control.

From where I stood at the window, I could see my bicycle. The plastic bag I'd used to cover the seat had blown off, I noted glumly. Again, the urge to get on my bike and ride home, see for myself that husband and home were okay.

I had been getting around by bicycle, despite the heavy rain. The few remaining open roads were clogged with cars. Driving was impossible. I had had to change my route almost daily, as roads, city blocks, and finally whole sections of town went under water. I carefully encased all of my stuff - a change of clothing, lunch, papers, in several layers of plastic bags before putting them into my panniers. Water got into everything anyhow. At night, I pored over maps, seeking out new routes on higher grounds. Day by day, my commute grew longer and hillier, as these new paths inevitably took me higher into the hills around the river.

Earlier today, as I went through unfamiliar terrain in the early morning light, I had found a creek swollen to cover the footbridge I needed to cross. I dismounted, walked my bike along the path where the bridge ought to be, and then set out resolutely into the muddy waters, unable to see my feet, unknowing how deep the water was. I edged my way to the other side, remounted, only to find the path again submerged about a mile farther ahead, this time for as far as the eye could see.

As I prepared to reverse my steps, I saw two cyclists walking their bikes out of the tall grass to my left. They had stopped and we exchanged information. They gave me directions to the route they had found, a way around. This proved to be a long slog through long grass concealing ankle-high water. When I finally got back on the trail and followed it to the next road, I found a sign, "Trail Closed." No way I could make it back through the dark. That path probably didn't even exist any more. Inundated. I would need to find another way to get home tomorrow. And, anyway, I had traumas to take care of. I tried to call home again. No service.

* * *

The old lady was done with her scans and ready to go up to SICU. She'd been put temporarily in Trauma #2 to make room for the stab wound.

"Come on Katie," Bob said to the med student, get your gloves, we'll suture her forehead lac."

"6-0 nylon. Leave nice long tails. Or somebody'll be cussing you out in clinic when it's time to remove them."

"Remember when Jenny put that whole row of staples down that guy's forehead - right down the middle – the attending was so pissed. Well, the guy <u>was</u> a drunk, but <u>still</u>."

The ER doc stuck his head in the cubicle. "There's a 40 year old female who was drunk and fell downstairs, head injury, hemothorax. They'll both get here at the same time."

"Naturally. You take the head injury, I'll take the stab." The backup Chief arrived, looking exhausted.

"My wife killed me today. Sandbagging all day..."

"Your house OK?"

"Oh yeah, but down the street..."

A clatter, a gurney and a group of people rushing down the hallway towards them.

"Incoming!"

"Which one?"

"Stab wound."

"In here. Feet first."

The stab wound was bad, I could see from where I stood. It wasn't just one stab, for starters. The man had been slashed, hacked, cut – hands and forearms, defensive wounds, it looked like, even a couple to the torso, it was hard to tell with all the blood. So much for "he fell on his own knife." Big knife, too, from the size of some of the stabs.

"Chest x-ray, couple of large-bore IV's, sample to the blood bank – 6 units, and let's get him to the OR." *Damn! I should have told them to take him straight to the OR from the helipad. Bypassed the ER completely.* But most of the time that was unnecessary, even counterproductive. Who could have known? Stab wound, they said, most of those were minor injuries. Someone had a gift for understatement.

"Come on, people, I want him in the OR in five minutes. Ten minutes max." His blood pressure hovered around 60, heart rate 140.

"How much fluid?"

"That's his fourth liter of Ringer's."

"Hang two units of O-neg. And tell the blood bank to hurry. He's bleeding out. Must have gotten something big." *Aorta. Vena cava. Portal vein. Iliacs. Liver. Put the knife in and twisted, maybe; or slashed.* The team was already staunching the bleeding from all the other wounds, the slashes, leaving just the deep stab to the abdomen to deal with.

I looked at the man's torso – one stab wound, almost 2" long, just under his right rib cage. Another, more like a slash, across his midriff, just above the umbilicus. The man was slender, with vaguely Oriental features. Young – mid-twenties, I guessed. Good. A strong young heart.

"Blood pressure's 90."

"Your chest x-ray's out."

I looked at the film. Both sides of the chest looked OK. Lung markings out to the periphery, no blood, no air. "Doesn't need a chest tube. OK, let's go," I said loudly, my voice harsh with the necessity of making myself heard over the din. "Let's go. Time to go. Let's go let's go let's go."

* * *

In the OR, we found a hole in the guy's liver big enough to stuff my fist into. Everything else was OK. We packed it, stopped the bleeding, and put a temporary closure on his abdomen. Wheeled him around to the SICU to stabilize. Damage control surgery. When I was a resident, back in the dark ages, we'd have kept working to stop the bleeding with sutures or clips, often until the patient had gotten 30 or 40 units of blood, often past the point of no return. Just pack it and come back in a day or two. Often the body takes care of itself.

No patients were brought in from the house fire. The scuttlebutt in the ER was that it was actually an abandoned apartment complex, and that arson was suspected. Insurance fraud. I knew the building in question. It was easily five blocks away from our home, and it was surely no loss to see it go.

It was too late to try calling Jonathan again, so I settled in for a couple of hours sleep. When I woke up, the sun was shining and cell phone service had been restored, although the lines were stilled jammed. I took a shower, and an hour later I was able to get through on my cell phone.

Two days later, the water started to recede, leaving behind mud, debris, and a monumental pile of wet sand bags. In the SICU, the trauma patients from my call night slept in deep sedation, on ventilators. It was really too early to assess the damage.

INTENSIVE CARE

I was driving home from the hospital, left hand slapping the steering wheel in time with the beat of "Born to be wild", when I almost hit the skunk ball. I mean "ball" in the sense of a mass of skunks, not in the sense of a skunk cotillion – at least I don't think that was what they were doing in the middle of the road. I'd just finished helping the team do an appendectomy on a healthy young college student – basically cured him, how often do you get to say that? – and it was only 10 p.m.

The skunks were almost in the middle of my lane of traffic. Before I could figure out exactly what was in my lane, I slammed on the brakes and floored the clutch. I braced myself for a rear-end collision from the tail-gating SUV behind me, but it didn't come. That driver was probably muttering, "Crazy female driver!" There, square in my low beams, was a whirling mass of white and black, furry tails and stripes, circling around and around each other in a frenzy. It was maybe the diameter of the top of a small bar table, the kind with three or four high stools around it. It reminded me of the ball formation small fish sometimes assume to delude a predator, to make themselves look larger and less edible.

There were two adults, and an uncountable number of half-grown ones, and the rapid churning of the ball was barely inching them collectively toward the shoulder. Generating a lot of heat but no light, as we sometimes say to the surgery residents when they are all talk and no action. There was no way to urge them to move faster. I was periodically almost blinded by the headlights of cars in the oncoming lane. All tails were raised, and I wondered if I would have to park the car outside when I got home. I felt and immediately quashed a strong impulse to get out of the car and shoo them off the road into safety. As soon as they were far enough over onto the shoulder, I slowly eased off on the clutch and pulled away, still unsure what I had just seen.

When I was ten years old, my family took me to Nantucket to see a complete solar eclipse. All the hotels were full, so we spent the night before the eclipse on the beach. I slept lightly, partly because of anticipation of the next day, and partly because the sand was cold and lumpy under my sleeping bag. Sometime after midnight, I awoke, lifted my head, and looked out into the fog around me. A single skunk marched very deliberately perhaps two feet in front of me, and disappeared into the sea mist.

The skunk encounter seemed like a dream the next day. No one else had seen the animal. My father helped me set up a pinhole camera so that we could watch the beginning and end of eclipse safely. As the moon started to occult the sun, he crossed his hands with fingers outspread and showed me how the spangles of light that came through the gaps turned into crescents on the sand. As the light withdrew, the temperature dropped and the seagulls fell silent, just as he said they would. At totality, we looked through exposed photographic film directly at the sun's corona for a minute or two, before the diamond ring effect signaled a need to return to the pinhole camera. The light grew, the temperature rose, and the gulls began to cry again. Over the years, I remembered the eclipse, but gave little thought to the skunk. Now I was again reminded of that nocturnal encounter.

I work in a semi-rural environment, and I see a lot of wildlife just getting to and from work, but I had never seen a skunk ball. I'd never even seen a single skunk in the middle of a busy street in the center of town. Most likely, this group had been displaced by the spring floods. But during idle moments in my normally busy life, I found myself remembering the skunks.

* * *

One week later I was on call again, and I was asked to see an elderly man in the medical intensive care unit. The MICU. Seventy eight years old, critically ill, and the question before me was: did he need an operation? I walked slowly around the foot of the bed, as if approaching him from another side might make things look better. From this new angle, the man looked even worse, if possible. I could see the frail muscles between his ribs retracting with each breath as he strained for air, sucking for more than even our best ventilator could deliver.

I placed my right hand on his swollen belly, wishing that I could see inside. The skin was stretch taut, almost shiny with tension. He groaned at my touch. He was too sick to send for x-rays or scans. I closed my eyes, shutting out the rest of the world and trying to will every ounce of sensitivity into my hands. *It's just you and me now. Tell me what's wrong with you. What should I do?*

Leaving my hands there, I opened my eyes and looked up at the vital signs display. His blood pressure hovered at shock levels, his flagging heart chemically whipped, blood vessels squeezed beyond endurance to channel the feeble stream of circulating blood toward the brain, and back to the heart. Maintain perfusion to brain at all costs. The rest of the body might be dying by inches, but the brain and heart must get blood. Now the bowel, perhaps, was dying. If so, it had to come out, or it would slowly and surely poison the rest of the body. But if the bowel weren't dead, then the stress of surgery might kill him. Even if the surgery were needed, he might not survive.

I turned away. A month or so ago, I had made the wrong decision. An old man, much like this old man, had died in the operating room while I resected several feet of dead, black, nearly perforated colon from his abdomen. I tried not to be influenced by my most recent case – evidence-based medicine was the mantra of the day. And that meant the medical literature – randomized clinical trials – not your last case, or your last few cases, or, even worse, your "experience." But experience lingered in your bones, in your hands. My hands remembered the feel of his eggshell ribs breaking under the force of my chest compressions giving him CPR, trying to force the blood to circulate.

I had gotten that patient back once, twice, and we'd been actually closing the abdomen when his heart stopped for the third time. His heart had been racing at 120, a fast beep-beep-beep that registered in the periphery of my consciousness, when I heard the cadence abruptly slow into the normal range. I remembered how the inside of his abdomen grew slightly cool under my gloved hands as we worked. Then the beeps faltered, and the alarm shrilled as his heart rate fell below the critical threshold value. I had stopped sewing, the frantic movement of my hands stilled for an instant, to look at the cardiac monitor. Heart rate 60, then 40, then 30… I hadn't waited for it to stop. I'd pumped on his chest again, confident I could pull him back from the brink again, but this time he had been well and truly gone, and I had to back away, finally, stripping my gloves as I left, kicking the door on the way out, leaving my resident to sew up. Going out to talk to the family.

Now I dreaded a repeat of the same scenario. And consciously fought my revulsion – that almost superstitious dread of a death in the OR – so that I might see clearly what the proper course of action was in this case. I opened my eyes and stepped back, lifting my hands.

Stalling for time, I went over the ICU flow sheet. Hourly records of pulse, blood pressure, urine output, labs, at least 20 parameters. In the end, it all came down to judgment. I looked up. Janet, my chief resident, stood facing me, concern evident on her open Midwestern face. Ready to do battle with this belly with me, ready to go into the OR and do whatever I told her to do. I fell back on the Socratic method.

"So, Janet, what do you think we should do?" *Unfair, unfair – if I don't know the right course of action, how can I expect her to know?*

"Well, he could have dead bowel. The lab work's consistent. And he's not making urine..."

"Yes. He could."

"But he sure is in bad shape..."

"So what should we do? What will you do, next year, when you're out in practice, and they call you to see a patient like this?"

I looked past Janet at that moment and saw Dr. Singh, the man's cardiologist, approaching. Singh was a tall, gentle Sikh with a turban, a polished steel bracelet, and an Oxford accent.

"Just a moment," I said, and motioned for him to join their discussion.

"Let us leave the bedside," Singh suggested mildly, gesturing at the patient. For all intents the patient seemed oblivious, but for all we knew, he might be listening. Chagrined, Janet and I followed Singh to a quiet area near the nurses' station.

"What is your assessment?" Singh asked. Always direct, no preliminary pleasantries. I was glad Singh was this man's doctor.

"He could have dead bowel, but he's really basically got terminal vascular disease. Dry black gangrene of his fingers and toes. And that's like having cancer..." I was reasoning through it step-by-step as I spoke, and the correct answer was coming to me with this stepwise reasoning. "He's dying by inches," I continued. "His heart is barely pumping – and even if we could get him through surgery – but I don't think we can – even if we can..." I felt, once again, those ribs breaking under my hands during the unsuccessful resuscitation attempt, just weeks earlier. My fingers flexed, and I just shook my head. I felt the corners of my mouth draw out, firming my lips, an automatic gesture of resolve.

"Then let us go and talk to his wife, shall we?"

I nodded.

A young nurse led the way to a small conference room outside the unit. The wife, a slender, white-haired woman in a periwinkle blue sweater, waited with a younger woman. Their daughter, perhaps. Both looked up as I entered, and the younger woman flipped her cell phone shut.

I introduced myself. Dr Singh had taken care of this man for a long time, and I saw their faces relax slightly when he followed me into the room. Stalling for time, I sat down slowly in a chair next to the wife. Her name was Gladys. I went through an explanation of our assessment of his situation, explaining carefully the options and the likelihood of a bad outcome regardless of the action taken. Trying, as always, not to sway the decision. Gladys had to be able to live comfortably with whatever action she chose. Years from now, in the dark, lonely nights of widowhood, there must be no regrets.

There was a long pause when I finished speaking. I left them alone with the chaplain for a while, saying that I would come back soon.

Outside, I went to the staff lounge and poured myself a cup of sour coffee. I sat cradling the paper cup in both hands, hunched over, inhaling the vapors. For no particular reason, I thought about my dad.

* * *

Dad had been a nuclear physicist employed by the government. Did he work on the Manhattan Project? Was he one of those who built the bombs that were dropped on Hiroshima and Nagasaki? No, but like every physicist of his generation, he had applied for a job with the project and would have been proud to be part of the action.

He worked as a civilian scientist at a local army base. Security was more lax in those days, and he often took me to his lab on weekends. There I saw, up close and personal, the massive particle accelerators that simulated radiation from a bomb. He showed it all to me, explained how the machines worked and how everything was named for earlier physicists. The Van de Graaf generator, Tesla coils, the Curie – named for a woman! Showed me how to read a dosimeter. How to do a wipe test, to see if any isotopes were left on a surface if radioactive materials had been handled in the area.

I was an only child, and I sometimes wonder if he would have preferred a son. If so, he never let on. He taught me how to hammer a nail straight and true. How to use a cross-cut saw. How to countersink nailheads and fill them in with putty, so that they would be nearly invisible on the finished project. He taught me that sawdust could explode. How to relight a pilot light, if it went out. How to fix a toaster, taking care not to damage the fragile translucent panels of *Isenglas*. Where the fuse box was. How to tell a blown fuse. How to change a fuse. Why it was bad to substitute a penny for a fuse. How to gap a spark plug. How to fix things with coat hanger wire, duct tape, and a soldering iron. How to solder things properly, so you didn't get a bad join. How to make a crystal radio. What a cat's whisker was.

When I decided to go to medical school, he told me it was just trade school. He thought I should become a mathematician because that was "a nice clean career for a woman". It wasn't that common in those days for women to enter either career. He respected my decision and came to my graduation ceremony with pride. I remember going to <u>his</u> graduation ceremony.

Both he and my mother had had to interrupt their own educations to earn money for their families during the Great Depression. When my mother first met the man who would be her life-long love, he was standing on a street corner in Philadephia, with a tripod and a simple box camera. He told her that he was waiting for an accident to happen, so that he could get a photograph and sell it to the <u>Inquirer</u>. She brought him home for dinner, and her mother said, "Don't you feed that man! If you feed him, we'll never get rid of him." I have a photo of my parents from about that time. He was dapper, in a suit jacket, shirt and tie, white bucks. His jacket, although clean, looked a bit lumpy, as if it had been washed and dried many times, or perhaps cut down to fit him after someone else discarded it. She wore a frilly printed blouse and shorts with embroidered suspenders in a sort of Alpine look that she had undoubtedly hand-made.

He went back to college first, getting his BA, his master's, and finally his PhD from Temple University. It was his PhD graduation ceremony that I remember. This was in the 1950's.

Shoe stores had x-ray machines that you could put your feet into and see how your shoes fit. You could stand there as long as you wanted, watching your toes wiggle. My father never let me put my feet in the machine. He told me that some of the earliest scientists had gotten sick from radiation, and it was only later that people started to realize the dangers.

He had done his PhD thesis on Cherenkov radiation – that beautiful blue glow in the depths of swimming pool nuclear reactors, charged particles going too fast through water, the swimming pool from hell – working under Dr Hans Breuer, a scientist who had been airlifted from Germany at the end of WWII. "They asked us for milk for their children," was all my father would say about those days. Hans would bring a large loaf of rye bread to the lab and slice a hunk from it every day for lunch, making that single loaf last several weeks. Once, he cut into a loaf that contained a dead mouse. Hans and my dad reckoned that the mouse had eaten its way in and suffocated in there. Hans threw away the part of the loaf that contained the dead mouse, but ate the rest.

While my father got his education at Temple, we lived with my mother's mother in a town just across the river from Philadelphia. My grandmother never swerved from her initial assessment that he wasn't worth feeding, but she cooked supper for all of us every night. We lived an uneasy truce in the small house. With the PhD, dad was able to land that job at the army base. It was in a nearby state. Always cautious, he worked there for a year, living in a rooming house, before moving his family. My mother kept working in Philadelphia, and my Grandmother minded me. My mother told me, years later, that she had cried for a week when they decided to move in with my Grandmother. When we moved away from that house, I was eight years old. I raged and wept. We took Grandmother with us. She and my dad never really got on – I'd hug my dad, and look around his shoulder to see her making faces at me. When I hugged her, he did the same.

When I was in high school, my dad and several other scientists got together and founded a community college. The first few years, the college held classes at night in a local high school. I often went with him, filling his pipe with aromatic damp tobacco that stained my fingers, so he could smoke as he drove. I sat in on classes of four or five earnest middle-aged male students, workers at local plants who wanted to get their college degrees so they could get better work. The courses in those days were all geared toward a technical education. Physics, chemistry, mathematics, circuits…all taught by four or five scientists, including my father.

Meanwhile, my mother went back to college, getting her BA and her master's from Johns Hopkins at night. Father drove her there for classes, and I generally went along for the ride. He and I would visit the university book store, where the brick steps were hollowed from generations of students, and wait for her in big shabby leather chairs in a student lounge. He would drowse while I worked on my homework.

After I went away to college and then medical school in a distant state, the community college prospered and grew. Land was bought and a fine campus sprung up in the rolling hills. The curriculum expanded beyond the practical technical courses into areas like sociology, psychology, literature. After my father retired, my mother taught there; she came from a generation of women who didn't drive, smoke, or drink; so my father drove her to her evening classes. I don't ever remember seeing them apart.

My father died in an intensive care unit almost five years ago. His health had been frail for a long time when, one night, my mother awoke around 2 am to feel him jerking rhythmically in the bed beside her. She turned on the light and realized that he was having a seizure. By the time I got there from the distant state where I was working, he was intubated and unresponsive. He never woke up.

As the days went by, my mother and I sat side by side on plastic chairs outside the small ICU in our local hospital, waiting for periodic visiting hours. People kept coming by – respiratory techs, LPN's – either to thank my mom for teaching them, or to tell her that my dad had taught them. That he had helped them get where they were today.

My mother had total faith that he would come back home with her, but I had seen the CT scans of his brain and knew that there would be no meaningful recovery. I prayed that I would not have to say it was time to disconnect him from the respirator. Mercifully, things took a turn for the worse and he slipped away on his own.

* * *

I drank the last of the coffee without tasting it, and got up. Singh was sitting at the small desk just outside the conference room, and he accompanied me to the conference room. I started to present the situation again, in different words. Sometimes people don't understand the first time.

But Gladys shook her head slightly from side to side – no. "He can't even hold his pen. He was a minister, you know. Always wrote his sermons longhand. What kind of life does he have? What does he have to look forward to? We should leave him in God's hands. No surgery," She said firmly.

I am never sure what to say at this point. Whatever the decision is, it is the right decision, because it is made with love. This time I heard the perfect words for this situation, coming from the physician sitting next to me.

"He is better in God's hands than he is in our hands," Dr. Singh said gently.

Unnoticed, I softly edged out the door. Outside, my team was waiting. Residents, medical students, nursing students. It's good form in a situation like this to debrief the team. To make teaching points about what has just happened. And, strangely, it brings a certain clarity to one's own thoughts.

I took a deep breath and looked around the circle of six or seven young faces and suddenly remembered that skunk family. I realized then that the adults were simply trying to herd the group off the road, kind of like sheep dogs circling a flock of sheep. I wondered if they had made it to safety.

THE MAKING OF A SURGEON

Surgeons use their hands as well as their brains (and hearts) to care for their patients. The invasive nature of the surgical specialties distinguishes them from the purely medical disciplines, such as neurology. These stories detail the world of the general surgeon. General surgery is a specialty unto itself. It is also a gateway to further training in pediatric surgery, plastic surgery, vascular surgery and many other subspecialties.

Ten years ago, I might have said that the primary tool used by the surgeon was the scalpel and that the surgeon's home was the operating room, and that that is how you tell a surgeon apart from the rest of the specialists. Now, as treatment has evolved, surgeons also employ endoscopic, endovascular, and medical tools as well as the scalpel.

There is a huge demand for general surgeons, and it is a very satisfying career. Many people who choose the surgical specialties enjoy other activities which use their hands or body – such as athletics, art, or music. Surgery has aptly been called a "body contact sport"

When we recommend surgery and take a patient to the operating room, we change that person's life forever, most often for the better. We see whether or not what we did – the work of our hands – was successful. We live in a very real way with our successes and our occasional failures. Surgeons need to be able to make decisions under conditions of (often) incomplete information, and most surgeons crave the immediate gratification of success or failure. Most surgeons are distinguished by a buoyant optimism and high energy level.

General surgery residency is a minimum of five years after graduation from medical school. Many residents choose to take additional years of research or specialty training. Almost half of the students who choose general surgery now are women. Most of our residents, male or female, are married and many have young children. It is a myth that you cannot do both. You need to be well-organized and to have a lot of energy and a sympathetic spouse.

GLOSSARY

Axilla – the space under the arm (the armpit). The axilla contains lymph nodes to which breast cancer may spread.

Chest tube - a tube placed into the chest to drain air or blood to treat a pneumothorax or hemothorax.

Coagulopathy – an abnormal bleeding tendency that can be hard to correct.

Colostomy – an operation in which part of the colon is brought out through the skin. Bowel contents are then evacuated into a bag which is removed, cleaned, and replaced as needed by the patient.

Diffuse axonal injury – a severe type of blunt head trauma in which the force of the injury breaks fiber tracts in the brain.

Eschar – the leathery firm inelastic layer of dead tissue and debris that covers a chronic wound or full-thickness burn.

Estrogen receptors – markers used to determine if a breast cancer responds to female hormones.

Evisceration – protrusion of bowel through a wound in the skin.

Ex-fix – external fixation device – a frame placed around a limb so that a broken bone may be stabilized. Screws anchor the broken bone directly to the external frame.

Gamma probe – a detector used to find radioactive nodes in the operating room.

Hemicolectomy – removal of half of the large intestine (colon), often performed for cancer.

Hemothorax – blood in the chest.

Hyperemia – dilated small blood vessels, often in response to lack of blood and oxygen.

Laparotomy – performing an operation to open the abdomen and gain access to its contents.

Lymph nodes – collections of white blood cells organized into little kidney bean-shaped clumps. Lymph nodes form part of the body's defense against bacteria and tumor cells.

NG tube – nasogastric tube – a flexible tube placed down the nose into the stomach to remove stomach contents.

Omentum – a sheet of fatty tissue that hangs down in the front of the abdomen like a fatty apron. Often called "the policeman of the abdomen" because it helps contain infection.

Pneumothorax – collapsed lung. A hole in the lung allows air to escape into the chest.

Pubis – the lower end of the abdominal wall at the pelvic bones.

Pulse oximeter – a clip placed on the patient's finger or ear lobe to measure how well oxygen is getting into the blood.

Ringer's Lactate – a solution of various salts used to resuscitate patients in shock.

Saphenous vein – a large superficial vein of the leg.

Thrombosed – clotted.

TRAM flap – transverse rectus abdominis flap – a reconstructive procedure in which tissue from the lower abdomen is transposed up into the mastectomy defect.

Xiphoid – the end of the breast bone, just above the abdomen.